Tesla's Imprint

Kimberly Adkins

New Orleans
2014!

Tesla's Imprint

Kimberly Adkins

Black Lyon Publishing, LLC

TESLA'S IMPRINT
Copyright © 2014 by Kimberly Adkins

Our books may be ordered through your local bookstore or by visiting the publisher:

BlackLyonPublishing.com

Black Lyon Publishing, LLC
PO Box 567
Baker City, OR 97814

This is a work of fiction. All of the characters, names, events, organizations and conversations in this novel are either the products of the author's vivid imagination or are used in a fictitious way for the purposes of this story.

Cover Model: Jason Aaron Baca.

ISBN-10:   1-934912-64-6
ISBN-13: 978-1-934912-64-5
Library of Congress Control Number: 2014938372

Published and printed in
the United States of America.

Black Lyon Contemporary Romance

To my dear friend Nappen, wherever you are. I'd like to think you're out there, somewhere, living a mysterious and exciting life like the characters in my stories.

ONE

"Do not make a sound. If they discover me, we'll both be in dire straits." His voice was soft and low, like a gentle caress. His clean-shaven cheek pressed against her throat in the confines of the small space.

She attempted to control her heartbeat, afraid the pulse pounding through her system might agitate the stranger. He'd mysteriously appeared in the ladies room with no warning.

The stall was small and dark, cramped by even old world standards. She could feel the cold tile wall against the naked skin of her exposed thigh between her skirt and stockings. He snapped off the light a moment before he burst into her cubicle, and though she thought herself familiar with European customs, Tess was quite certain that this type of intrusion was not appropriate in any kind of venue. Still, he hadn't hurt her and stranger things than this had happened to her during a night on the town.

He cocked his head to the side to listen before he relaxed his posture and she was able to move a little inside his arms.

"I apologize for the rather abrupt meeting. Your stall was marked as unoccupied and I had a bit of a run-in with some unfriendly types in the alleyway."

"The alley is outside. We're inside … and two stories off the ground, I might point out." She wasn't sure why he bothered to offer an explanation, but he could have tried to make some sense if he was going to do it.

"Right on all accounts." His deep, smooth voice answered her with infinite patience.

"Then how did you get—"

"I'm terribly sorry. My manners have obviously gone right out the window." He cut her off instantly, the tone of his voice slightly amused. "May I inquire after your name?"

"Tesla," she answered, and was embarrassed by the proper response she saved only for her academic instructors. "Oh, I despise that name—it's so ridiculous. Everyone calls me Tess."

His weight shifted a small amount in the closed space and she was acutely conscious of his clean, musky scent.

"Wait a second. Why am I explaining myself to you?" she whispered boldly. "Get out of here right now or I will scream and alert the alley-hopping, levitating bad guys chasing you. Oh yes, and I imagine the night watch security will come, too."

"Your parents were scientists?" He asked in response to her name, as if he hadn't heard her threat. Despite her better judgment, his soft tone weakened her guard.

"I don't mean to be rude," she answered him, her American accent coming through despite her previous attempt to sound cultured. "But who the hell are you and why are you in the bathroom with me?"

Before Tess could draw a breath to follow through with her earlier promise, a swift, firm finger flew to her lips and touched them together in silent resolve. The action was so gentle and intimate that she was immediately stunned into silence.

Tess had been trying in vain to make out any of her captor's features in the darkness of their enclosure. Now she found it was possible to discern the shape of his strong jaw line and the curve of his mouth when he spoke.

"I apologize again for taking up so much of your time, but I am grateful for your understanding and kindness. I'll just be on my way now."

He popped the latch and slipped out the door, attempting to close it behind him as she stood inside.

"Wait!" She braced the swinging stall door with her hand to follow him out into the main part of the powder room.

Even in the more spacious area it was still a little dark in the building, but she knew that was because the entire night club was lit by soy candles. It was their trademark and one of the reasons she loved coming there so much.

"You don't want to take me hostage or anything, fumble around for cab fare in my purse ... nothing like that?"

He stopped before he reached the outer door and she was able to see how tall he was in his perfectly tailored black tuxedo. His hair was very dark, maybe black, and came down to the white collar inside his suit. Her heart skipped a beat when he turned to face her and he offered her a half-smile in the candlelight.

"I'm afraid I'm late for the opera, my dear." His eyes reflected the flickering flames all around them and they appeared to be a beautiful shade of dark blue.

He reached into his pocket to search for something, breaking eye contact. Tess turned to her shadowy reflection in the mirror while he was distracted, smoothing her unruly red curls over her shoulders as she struggled for something to say that would give him pause.

Her mystery man swiftly removed what Tess thought was a flashlight at first, though she quickly realized that wasn't the purpose for the strange object. He gripped the base of the copper cylinder with his right hand and turned the rim along the top in a clockwise motion until it clicked, and then back the other way. It appeared to be some type of combination lock.

Did he have a bomb? Was everyone inside the club in danger?

Tess was right behind him when he exited into the corridor. Flickering candles struggled in their wall sconces as they passed until one flame after the other snuffed out. She shivered, thinking the temperature out in the hall was at least twenty degrees cooler than the rest of the bar. Maybe it was because the candles went out, but the warm colors of the wood paneling in the hall took on a shallow, cold hue and it was like something she'd see in a horror movie late at night.

"They're scanning for me. The remote tracking device takes all the surrounding energy in the area to power itself as it passes through. I thought they had gone, Tesla. I'm sorry, but they may have caught you in the sweep. It wasn't my intention to involve anyone else in this."

Before she could sputter out any questions he strode boldly to the place where she was standing, taking her hand and forcing her away from the advancing darkness.

"We must go to a place where there are a lot of people. We'll mingle until the scan has passed and all the collective energy will throw them off for certain." He slipped his arm around her waist like it was a natural thing to do, pulling her very close to his side.

Tess took a moment to consider she might be going crazy. She definitely saw something back there in the hallway, but she was pretty sure that crazy people see things all the time that seem real to them.

"This way to the dance floor, the club is packed tonight. If you want to lose yourself in a crowd, this is the best place in London to do it."

The entire establishment echoed with the throbbing sound of music. As she led him down the stairs it grew louder and began to pulse inside her skin and the hair on the back of her neck stood on end. As they skirted the edge of the dance floor looking for a place to cut in a familiar voice caught her attention.

"Tess! Where have you been? We almost came looking for you. That cute guy you've been eyeing at the end of the bar said he'd buy you a drink if you danced with him."

Sophie tugged on her sleeve, her brilliant smile filled with excitement for Tess's big score. It took a moment for her friend to realize that she was attached to the tall, dark and handsome man at her side, but when she did her jaw dropped.

"Sophie, stop it!" Tess struggled to raise her voice over the crowd. "That's hardly polite."

Her blue-eyed escort released his hold on her waist and faced Sophie solidly before taking her hand in his.

"You may tell the 'cute guy' at the end of the bar that this moment belongs to me." He smiled in such a charming manner that Tess was sure she saw her friend's knees shake as he kissed the back of her hand with slow intent.

Though he had spoken softly, every word carried across the small space with perfect clarity. Once he saw she understood his message, he turned his undivided attention back to Tess.

His arm was at her waist again, but this time she found herself pressed against the full length of his body and they were at the heart of the crowd before she knew it.

The music was dark and gothic in turn, and it sent shivers down her spine that her dance partner traced effortlessly with his fingertips. They were in the center of the throng but no one touched them as they slowly moved against each other to the languid, sensual beat.

The flashing lights overhead made her dizzy and she closed her eyes against the colorful pulses that played their patterns across her face. His arms were strong around her, and he held her against him protectively as he moved them closer to the mirrored wall along the edge of the dance floor.

"You have such lovely, pale skin. Look at you, my dear."

Tess opened her eyes and gazed at her reflection in the mirror. Her light blue sweater and pleated skirt had seemed cute earlier in the evening as she and her college roommate dressed for one last night on the town. Now, next to the exquisite stranger at her side, she felt like a little school girl and not the grown woman who had just received her university degree.

As she watched their reflection, she felt his fingers gently stroke her wayward curls and though she could have sworn she felt him lightly kiss her cheek, his image in the glass made no such movement.

Tess didn't know what was real at the moment, but she knew what she wanted it to be. Disregarding their image she turned to her dance partner and faced him. With careful, calculated movements she stood on tiptoe to feel the front of his thighs against hers and lifted her face to his, lips parted as she settled a delicate kiss on his smooth chin.

His smoky eyes were dark, his lids half-hooded as he endured her innocent attempt at seduction. Her heart pounded and she knew he had to feel it against his chest. She was as close as she could possibly be to him.

With slow determination he reached both of his hands behind her back and laid them on her shoulders as if he were going to pull her away, but at the last second he slid them down the curve of her spine until they came to rest on the small of her back.

"I should not do this," he whispered, though she wasn't sure if he was telling her or himself as his large hands spread out across her back. He pressed her against him with an all-encompassing hold she had never experienced before in her life.

The air was forced from her lungs in a startled gasp.

The moment her mouth opened he found her lips and kissed them with such deep, unrestrained passion that she responded to him on the most primal level of her being and returned to him the most ardent kiss her soul had to offer.

Tess was lost to the world during that moment where there seemed to be no time, no place, nothing but the perfect harmony of the universe for the two of them to exist in—and it was perfection. The kiss was so perfect that when he released her, she lost her balance and stumbled on the dance floor.

Their song had finished, but nothing followed its play. She finally noticed everyone staring at her as she stood alone, pressed against the mirror for support. Sophie came to her side and put her arm around her shoulders, looking as confused as everyone else when she brushed the hair from Tess's eyes.

"Did you see him Sophie? Am I crazy?"

"I saw him—at least I remember that I did. I think he went out the front door, but then I forgot what I was doing. I feel so dizzy."

The crowd started muttering and yelling for the DJ to play some tunes, calling him a slacker, just as a handsome young fellow at the end of the bar began to complain loudly to the bartender that someone had knocked over the drink he bought for his future girlfriend.

"Wait here, Sophie. You're a little shaky at the moment. I just have to see for myself, okay?"

"I really don't think that's a good idea. We're not supposed to go anywhere alone this late at night. Besides, I still don't know what happened just a few minutes ago."

"I'm just going to look out the front door. If I don't see him, I'll come right back in and we can call it a night, agreed?"

"You have five minutes. Seriously, Tess, I mean it this time. Check in with Bruno in the lobby so he knows what's going on."

Her plea fell on deaf ears, because Tess was already running for the door. Either the bouncer had wandered off or it was late enough that he didn't need to mind the front any longer, but Tess sensed she had no need of protection.

She swept out into the street and the black asphalt was wet from a fresh rain. The lamplights sparkled off the pavement like diamond dust as she searched frantically for any sign of him. The sound of crisp leather soles echoed from the alley beside the club and she recalled what he jokingly said earlier about being in the alley when he encountered trouble. Perhaps he had gone back to the same spot!

Tess walked quickly to the side of the building and cut down the small access road that ran between the structures, the gutters dripping from the recent downpour. She stepped over the broken bricks and garbage until she saw him in the shadows.

"I knew it wasn't a good idea," he said quietly, and the sound of his voice carried to her over the short distance between them.

He took the copper cylinder from his pocket again, and this time she could see a series of flashing lights running in sequence along the top. He wore white dress gloves, his tuxedo now complete, and he wasn't fazed a bit by the ticking clockwork sounds from the now sparkling device.

"If you could just wait for a minute..."

"Stop." He held up a gloved hand when she dared to take two steps forward.

"I was wrong to engage you on the dance floor. I made a promise quite a long time ago and for good reason. Though I admit on this particular night, it bothers me more than I care to say."

She was silent as he turned to an alleyway door with an ordinary brass knob. Tess watched with dread as he attached the open end of the copper tube over the round handle, turning it carefully as the clockwork mechanism inside the cylinder whirred with an intense frenzy.

The chipped metal door swung out and a bright, orange light crept into the center of the alley. She edged closer to him, all the while holding his gaze and she could finally see how beautiful he was in the bright light.

He smiled at her, and a look of longing on his face mingled with regret as he stepped through.

Tess peered into the opening, the glare hurting her eyes, and it appeared that he had walked onto the rooftop of a beautiful city. The graceful, white wings of an amphitheater rose in the distance and something about it seemed strikingly familiar.

"Is that … is that Sydney?" She stumbled over the words, knowing her question was impossible, but not more so than the answer.

"I told you earlier, I'm late for the opera. Keep the door closed behind me, will you, love?"

Without another word, he pulled the rusted piece of metal shut and the latch clicked into place. The alley reverted to its original damp, dark state and Tess shivered from the sudden change in her environment.

"This is crazy, I know this is crazy," she repeated over and over again, as she reached out a trembling hand to grasp the same brass knob the stranger had turned before. The knob was almost unbearably warm to the touch and a lingering, acrid scent filled the air.

Even though she knew it was impossible, her eyes reflexively squinted closed as she pulled the door open with a rough, clumsy jerk. The smell of rotting wood and garbage greeted her from the stairs that led down into the dank cellar. There was no morning sun, no beautiful city at her feet and no sign of her handsome stranger in the darkness below.

The journalist inside her wanted to know more about the stranger and how he did it. There was never a story she couldn't press out the answers for at the university paper, but this situation was different. There was nothing left to investigate. She put her face in her hands and breathed deeply to calm herself. As she did, she realized the musky scent of his skin lingered on her fingertips.

•

Simon leaned with his back against the door. The metal was searing hot through his layers of clothing, but he barely reacted to the burn. He understood the feeling that flooded through his being, the sense that the young woman from the nightclub was just on the other side of the frame. It was false, of course. Once the device opened the slice it automatically detached and became inactive. When the door closed she was a world away.

What am I thinking? He firmly banged his head against the solid door, tacky with hot paint. When he'd told her he made a promise, he couldn't have been more serious—and more disturbed by his reaction to the encounter in the night club than he cared to admit to himself.

What could he possibly have to offer such a beautiful young woman after a dance like the one they shared? God, he didn't even know who he was. The only thing he could even be sure about was that he was in danger, all the time.

He had to learn the truth about his past and why he knew the things he did without remembering them. Until then, the only thing he could be is a shadow on the edge of society. Everyone was safer that way.

He replayed the way she felt in his arms, how she stood on her toes to kiss his chin with her irresistible lips. She felt familiar to him in a way he hadn't experienced for what seemed like a lifetime. It didn't matter, though. He couldn't let it matter. She was halfway across the world now, and all the better for it.

Besides, he had work to do.

Two

"We have a few weeks before the lease expires, you know." Sophie twisted a strand of her long, black hair between her fingers, a gesture that always gave her away when she was fretting over something serious. "You don't have to pack everything up all at once."

"That's easy for you to say, my friend." Tess placed her hands on her hips as she surveyed the transient mess she had made with tottering boxes and oddly shaped suitcases in her room. "You have an internship lined up already at the University so you don't have to go far. I, on the other hand, have no clue where I will land."

The idea she'd worked for so long to earn a graduate degree that didn't net her any job opportunities left Tess a little apprehensive about her future. A few internships at mid-level papers looks promising, but she'd hadn't gotten any firm offers. Unlike her best friend Sophie, she had no relatives to return to and no place to call home. Now that they were finished with school, she really couldn't borrow her friend's family any longer.

Tess drew a deep breath and brushed a few strands of loose curls away from her forehead. Perhaps it was due to the uncertain future on her horizon, but she had a difficult time letting go of the fantastic encounter she'd had at the nightclub the other evening. The image of the stranger's face haunted her thoughts whenever she let her guard down and allowed her mind to wander aimlessly. The whole experience was ridiculous, of course. Everything that happened could easily be explained away with ideas of hypnosis, someone slipping a Mickey into her drink or even the odd layers of smoke in the air.

Dammit though, I can still feel his skin against my lip—and there is no way that didn't happen.

"I thought the whole condition of your secret trust fund hinged on the premise that you would work at the company your parents founded before you were born?" Tess sighed, pulled out of her romantic daydream. She threw her hands up in the air before sitting down heavily on the bed as Sophie navigated through the boxes on the floor to join her.

"You said it right there, sister. The word is secret. So my parents died in a lab accident when I was five years old. It's like something out of a comic book, you know? Whatever they were doing, I didn't have the security clearance to understand. I still don't know what that company is to this day and the only person I have ever seen was an old man in a deserted office building in New York. He summoned me there to sign papers when I was eighteen years old and then again when I was 21. The business probably went under years ago and no one could be bothered to tell me."

"I know, I remember when you went to New York." Her friend put a comforting arm around her shoulders. "It's not true that you don't have any place to go, though.

You have me. We have been roommates here for over eight years and it's sad that you don't know anything more about your past than you did when we started, but look at it in a positive light if you can. Your entire education was paid for and all your needs have been taken care of without question. You've even used the money you received to help me and my family survive more than once when times were difficult."

Tess looked good and hard at her friend next to her. Sophie came from a family with nine children. It was no secret they struggled to do simple things like put food on the table for them all, let alone send their eldest daughter to an Ivy League school. They were good people, though, and Sophie earned her tuition through hard work and scholarships. Still, it wouldn't have been enough if Tess hadn't befriended her early in their freshman year and developed such a close bond with the girl.

"You're right, of course. I should count my blessings instead of lamenting them. Life could have certainly thrown a lot more challenging things our way instead of setting us up in a cozy flat along the Thames while we attended a posh university with nothing to do but make our grades."

"Just do me one favor, okay?" Sophie looked up at her with her big, brown eyes and Tess thought her lower lip trembled a little bit.

"I might have a favor left in me, now that you mention it."

"Don't pack everything today. I can't handle it. Spread it out over the next few weeks so we can see what opportunities pop up for you in London. I just know we'll get to stay together."

"Sure, unless the Men in Black come knocking on

my door and present me with an offer I can't refuse." Tess laughed. It felt good to let some of the tension go that had been building up since graduation.

"Ha! As long as it's Will Smith, they can knock on my door any day," Sophie said, but her eyes widened in surprise as the doorbell to their flat chimed softly through the suite.

"You don't think …" Tess started, but let her words linger.

"That it's Will Smith? Gosh, he's early! I told him not to come until eight o'clock."

"You wish." Tess jumped up and straightened her sweatpants and T shirt, just to be proper. "Really though, I'm not expecting anybody."

"Me either. A girl can always dream, however."

They strolled to the door arm in arm and she felt like they were young again, just starting school together and going on a new adventure. For the first time since their final semester began Tess had hope that perhaps everything would be alright. She reached out and opened the door with a radiant smile on her face.

A young man stood in the hallway dressed in soft, faded jeans and a form-fitting black T-shirt. His light brown hair was shoulder-length, streaked with blonde. He ran a nervous hand through it to pull the hair away from his warm, hazel eyes.

"Not Will," Sophie said under her breath in Tess's direction, "But still not disappointing."

"No kidding," Tess whispered back, but her friend was already smiling and staring at the ceiling.

"Hi, I'm Ryan. You must be Tess Pelham." The young man reached his hand toward the taller girl as if he were expecting her to shake it, but she crossed her arms instead. He appeared to be genuinely distressed by her reaction.

"How do you know I'm not Tess?" Sophie took a step forward and joined her friend, hip to hip.

"My father said Tess was a redhead, and that she was very pretty." He nearly stuttered over his words before he glanced shyly at the dark-haired girl. "You're both very pretty, though."

"I think he likes you." Tess nodded to her friend and nudged her with a polite elbow.

"In that case, I think you'd better come in." Sophie gestured openly and backed away so he could enter the living room.

He smiled gratefully at her invitation, but then glanced over his shoulder as he left the hall. Something about his presence was out of order, though Tess couldn't quite put her finger on it.

"First of all, I want to congratulate you on behalf of PT for your accomplishment at the University. Your degree is impressive, just as you have become an impressive young lady in your own right."

"Me?" Tess gave him a puzzled frown, and he nodded to her with his own uncertain gaze. After his obviously rehearsed speech, he appeared to be at a loss for words.

"What is PT?" Sophie said just as it was beginning to feel uncomfortable. "Are you from some kind of recruiting firm or someone hoping to take advantage of new graduates at the University?"

"Um, I'm sorry. No one has told me how much you know, exactly. Please don't be upset with me, because I don't know a lot, either." Ryan ran his hand through his hair again before he awkwardly continued.

"PT is Poly Tech Acquisitions, Miss Pelham. It's your parents' foundation. I was asked to come here with your travel papers, so you wouldn't have to fly back to the States alone."

"Wait a minute." Sophie was on him with tears in her eyes before he could even blink. "You can't just walk in here and take away my best friend. Not like that! We don't even know who you really are. I don't think so, do you hear me?"

"Listen, Ryan," Tess said as she rested a soothing pair of hands on Sophie's shoulders. "You have to realize I haven't heard a word from this foundation in years. I've never met anyone from it except some crazy old man who sat behind a desk in some deserted high rise."

"That old man was my father, actually." Ryan looked down when he said it, and stray hair fell over his eyes again, hiding his emotions.

"He was supposed to come for you himself. I guess it was something he promised your parents long ago. When I said I didn't know a lot about this, I really don't. He told me who you were, gave me your arrangements and asked me to take his place. It was his last wish. He seemed excited that your day had come, so I thought you would be happy when we met."

"I was never even told your father's name, Ryan. Do you understand me?"

"No, I don't. Not really. I only visited him during the summers, but I know he kept a file with things about you in it. He would mention your scores at the university from time to time, maybe put a report or clipping of you inside a folder. He always said to me that your parents would have been proud."

"Did he work for Poly Tech? He barely said a handful

of words to me both times he met with me."

"I can't be certain if he did. Near the end, though, his mind wandered a little and he let his guard down when he spoke. He knew who they were and didn't care a lot for the establishment. He often mentioned his responsibility to your parents, and said it was important to protect your birthright. He never wanted me to speak to anyone else but him about you."

"The question is, Mister Bearer of Bad News, what was he protecting for her?" Sophie put her hands on her hips. "If you tell me you don't know, there's no way she's walking through that door without me. Somebody has to make sure everything's on the up and up."

"You have to start your internship soon, and your entire family is waiting for you to come home for the break." Tess turned earnestly to her closest companion. "Surely you don't want to follow me to some boring corporate office in the middle of a huge city, Sophie."

"Really?" her friend answered with a laugh. "Do you think I'm dying to go home before my job starts to spend two months squeezed into a bedroom with three of my sisters, while we draw numbers for whose turn it is to use the bathroom next? I'll pass, thanks."

"Actually, my father never specified that anyone else couldn't come. The jet is chartered already so another passenger wouldn't hurt as long as she has a passport."

"She has a name, my handsome young man and I'd like you to address me with more familiarity." Sophie took it upon herself to slip her free arm around their blushing messenger. At the same time she removed the files he was carrying and handed them to Tess, who addressed him with her own concern.

"Ryan?"

"Yes, Miss Pelham?"

"Do you think they even know I'm coming?"

•

"Seriously, what are we doing here?"

It was late in the afternoon and the deserted night-club had an entirely different atmosphere during the day. Still, the clean scent of the soy candles permeated every nook and cranny in the establishment. Tess gazed with unsuppressed longing at her reflection in the mirror that lined the polished floorboards where she had danced.

Sophie sent Ryan to the bar to procure a few drinks and give the two girls some time to talk about what they were planning.

"It's obvious what we're doing here, isn't it? We need to look over these documents before I leave to make sure they're legit ... and there is no sense being thirsty as we do."

"You're still on about that guy, aren't you—the magician in the tuxedo from the other night? In case you've forgotten, he left you on the dance floor. His disappearing act was rotten. They're never any good if they don't reappear again, you know."

Of course that was all Sophie remembered of him, and Tess had enough of her senses left that she hadn't mentioned the occurrence in the alleyway to her already skeptical friend. There really was no point, after all. Either she was crazy and he ditched her through a dimensional doorway, or she was crazy and he caught a cab and her mind made up the impossible exit.

"That's my point exactly," Tess said as she looked over her shoulder at Ryan who was caught staring at Sophie from the bar. "Maybe he'll reappear one time before I go. Besides, you've already gotten your admirer. Can't I have one last try for mine?"

"Ryan is really cute, isn't he? I usually don't attract that type. Of course, that's not the reason I want to come with you. This is all so mysterious. What if I let you go off alone and I never hear from you again? I'm not sure how I could live the rest of my life with any kind of good conscience."

"Well, that and you finally met a guy who can afford to pay our bar tab. You're sure your family doesn't mind?"

"My sisters jumped for joy when they learned they didn't have to move a fourth bed into their room for two months. Believe me, I'll be in far better comfort with you than I would be at home for the interim."

Finally convinced her friend was fine with the decision to accompany her to the United States, Tess sat back in her chair and closed her eyes. She wished she could tell her more about the strange encounter without sounding like a nut.

"His voice was so beautiful, Sophie. Deep and warm, it vibrated inside me when he spoke, like music. So we only had one dance, that's true, but how long does it take for your heart to realize that it has been beating since the day you were born to exist in that one perfect moment of completion?"

"Wow, Tess. I'm really sorry," her friend looked surprised by her confession. "I guess I didn't realize how important he is to you. I don't know why—maybe because you only saw him for five minutes. But, I really do think that if you believe so strongly in your heart's desire you will be given another chance."

Tess noticed Sophie's eyes glance toward Ryan as he

held their three drinks in his steady hands, his strong arms flexing to balance them so he didn't spill a drop.

"These papers, though ..." She changed the subject as he drew near. "None of them actually say Poly Tech on them except for the notes on the location. What do we really know about this establishment? Who runs it now? I'm not big into the stock market, but I'm pretty sure I've never seen them listed on an index anywhere."

"I noticed that, too." Ryan joined them at the small table and pointed to a list of the board of directors. "My father mentioned they were in acquisitions and when I asked what they acquired he said they bought, recovered and developed unusual technologies."

"So, you've never been there, either?" Sophie raised a brow in his direction. "When you're not running errands for Tess's estate, what do you do, exactly?"

"I admit I'm not really suited for this type of social interaction." He blushed under her direct stare. "I'm an archaeologist who specializes in ancient civilizations. Unfortunately, I seem to manage much better with the mysteries of the dead than the complex realities of the living."

"We'll see what we can do to advance your social skills, won't we?" Sophie leaned in and winked at her friend.

"I'm sure you will." Tess took a moment to regard the two people seated at the table with her. During the course of their study she had never really seen Sophie so interested in any man. Granted, this particular fellow carried an air of mystery even if he did it awkwardly, but his intentions appeared to be honest. Though she had no way to prove it, Tess could feel that it was so.

"Let me buy this round of drinks, for two best friends

from the University and one promising addition to the nest we build for our future." She raised her glass to the newcomer.

The two girls made their way toward the warm oak counter that shone in the candlelight of the exclusive club, growing more relaxed in Ryan's company. It was enjoyable to have free reign of the establishment in the off hours of operation.

"Lucky are we three," Sophie cheered as they all raised their glasses high. No sooner had the words left her lips than the door to the front foyer burst open, ushering in a cold breeze. They all turned toward the commotion, though the door swung shut again with no one coming through. Tess couldn't help but feel like secretive eyes were on the group and she wasn't the only one.

•

Thorns pricked his fingers, but the pain barely registered next to the feeling of elation Simon felt at seeing Tess again. How long had he lurked in the shadows with his blooming rose, waiting for just a glimpse of her again?

Are you out of your mind?

Simon harshly questioned his motives when he fully realized he was standing in a pub, stalking a beautiful young woman he had no business giving a second thought to. He'd never meant to come back there, never had a plan to see her again, yet here he was.

The truth was simple: she felt familiar to him. And being the selfish bastard that he was, desperate for any information about his past, he risked her life again by seeking her out to see if she struck the same nerve she had the night on the dance floor.

Oh, and she did. Seeing her here a second time

stirred some type of vague emotion he wasn't familiar with. How had he known her? She certainly hadn't recognized him.

He was sure no one tracked him here, though he knew without a doubt how dangerous it was to visit the same place twice. There was no other option, in this case. Simon could carry on as a rogue, searching for answers that he might never find, or he could grasp on to the one thing that had blinded him like a spark in the darkness.

If you do this, my friend, you must never let harm come to her because of your past—no matter what your past may be. Exchanging his old promise for this new one didn't sit well with his sense of honor, but it was all he could do.

He decided not to approach her at the bar. Her back was to the room and it might startle her. The best way to appear was to sit calmly at their table and wait. Even a second would feel like forever, but he had to be cautious.

No one noticed as he neared their belongings, carelessly tossed on top of the table where their empty glasses sweated on coasters.

How nice it would be to let down my guard like this, he thought. *Even not watching my back for an instant would be a luxury.* With a gentle hand he nudged one of their folders to the side before a pool of condensation could spread to its spine.

And he noticed the scribbling on the front. His heart pounded so hard he was afraid people could hear it on the street. He retrieved the manila folder with a shaky hand and saw the words written there—Poly Tech Acquisitions, Entry Codes and Procedures.

He glanced at the bar where the trio of friends was still engaged, though everything around him felt surreal now. He reached into his pocket and pulled out the copper cylinder, turning it over in his hands until the plating came into view.

Poly Tech Acquisitions was engraved on the handle. He opened the file and his eyes sped over the protocol listed there. This meant something—something that he knew in his heart was for him. There couldn't be a coincidence between his familiarity with Tess and his recognition of this name. And if that was true, she could be as dangerous to him as the dark clad men who hunted him.

Or, she could be in the same kind of danger herself.

There was no time to draw any kind of conclusion. His years of self-preservation kicked in when Tess turned away from the bar as if she might be heading back to the table. He dropped the rose without a thought and pulled a black plastic square from his pocket. The flower landed on the table amidst the paperwork, minus the folder he still clutched with his free hand.

He flipped the blinking chip into the center of his palm and looked at it. "I've never activated you twice in a row so quickly. Let's see what you can give me." Simon depressed a button on the interface of the object and ran for the front door of the night club.

•

"Perhaps it's best if you folks take your celebration to another pub." The red-haired vendor shifted uncomfortably at his post behind the ledge of polished wood, before superstitiously making the sign of the cross. He looked as if he had seen a ghost.

"Wow, throwing us out on so little, really? We truly

must be done with the London scene, my friends." Tess took the allotted amount for the bill and dropped it carelessly onto the bar in a pretense that barely covered her jitters. Whatever spooked the barman had her on edge too, but she still didn't take kindly to that kind of treatment.

"We'll just collect our things and be on our way to the limo that waits for us, right?" Sophie said over her shoulder as loudly as possible, but her glance fell on the table at the same moment as Tess. There was no mistaking the red rose lying on the spot where they previously enjoyed their glasses of wine.

"Did you see anyone come by our table?" Tess turned a pale face toward the bartender, and when he earnestly shook his head she looked to her friends.

"I'll just step outside to have them hold the car then?" Ryan took his papers off the table, pulling them out from under the rose like a parlor trick. He didn't seem to think much of the flower's sudden appearance. Instead, he focused on the stack of folders in his hands as he walked to the front.

"It's just a rose. Someone dropped it while they were cutting through to the alley in back." Sophie tapped the petals to make her point as Tess reached for the thick, green stem.

"There is no back door into the alley, the only way out would be through the windows in the bathroom."

"Well, how do you know that? Sit in on a lot of fire escape committees?"

"I just know. But you're right, of course. Someone dropped it and luckily for us, it landed on our things. Finders keepers, after all. It's still kind of romantic, though."

"It is," Sophie smiled and reached for the stem, but Tess found herself unwilling to let it go. "Let me hand it to Ryan, please. It will be so sweet!"

"You just met him, are you mad?"

"If I am, I might tell you it takes one to know one. It seems to me a certain young lady met a stranger just the other night, and after one dance has been mooning about for him ever since. Come on, you know I have a point."

Tess released the fragrant flower with a smile, knowing her savvy roommate had her dead to rights. Her encounter with the magician may not have blossomed into the fantasy that she dreamed about, but that was no reason Sophie shouldn't have a chance.

"I think you have a live one there on the line. Reel him in gently," Tess kidded her. They walked out of the dim interior of the club and into the foyer as the late afternoon sun streamed through the windows.

A brochure of some sort was caught between the glass doors. The top page of the exposed paper flapped in the wind and Tess's eye caught something familiar. Sophie had the bud pressed to her nose, unaware of her surroundings as she pushed the handle forward. Tess had to be quick on her feet to retrieve the pamphlet before it blew away.

Her knuckles turned white on the cover and her free hand reflexively flew to her mouth to stifle a gasp of surprise.

"Oh, look, it's the Sydney opera house," Sophie commented as she pointed to the clear picture on the page in Tess's hand. "What in the world is a program from Australia doing here, I wonder?"

She wanted to answer her friend, but couldn't even

begin to imagine where she should start. Before she was able to confide, Ryan rushed up to them on the sidewalk. His cheeks were flushed and his eyes wide with panic.

"We have a problem. I think I lost a file out of our paperwork and our flight is scheduled to take off in 55 minutes."

"Well, did you lose one or didn't you? Let's start there," Tess tapped her foot and watched as the town car pulled around the block to pick them up.

"It was with the other folders when we went in the club. I remember looking at it. But I must have lost it in there because it's nowhere to be found now."

"Was it something important? Do we need it? I didn't see anything left behind and I was the last one out."

"To be honest, I was going over the file again earlier because it contained instructions to arrive at our destination. They were so odd that I wanted to be sure I understood them correctly. There were all sorts of procedures and key codes. Not to mention a hand drawn map to the headquarters."

"So I'm guessing we can't Google the location, then?"

"Not unless you want the men in black showing up on your doorstep, I suspect. Well, I'll just have to inquire when we arrive. And you might want to pull your jackets out of your suitcases before we get on the jet. It will be rather chilly where we are going"

"It's not cold at all in New York during this time of year, Ryan. I packed most of my summer clothes."

"We're not going to New York, Miss Pelham, though you might want to change out of your sundress before we arrive. The mountains of Colorado can grow quite chilly late in the evening—even this time of year."

THREE

"But I thought we'd take in a few Broadway plays, maybe hit a piano bar or two before we went into some stuffy meeting with boring board members. I didn't realize this was going to be really off-Broadway."

It was the only explanation she had for Sophie as they stood over her open suitcase, pulling out one flimsy dress after another. Her dark-haired friend was ever practical, always with a sweater and sensible shoes, but she looked with longing on a silken blue sheath dress Tess had spread out on the bed when they started going through her things.

"I'll trade you this button-up cardigan for that," she offered, and Tess knew the girl had probably never worn anything like that gown before in her life.

"The way I see it," Sophie continued with a mischievous grin, "is we are stuck in the mountains with nearly no sign of civilization in sight. You'll have to hand over the dress if you don't wish to freeze!"

"I'd hardly call this resort uncivilized, though it's difficult to believe it's already off-season here. This place is beautiful. I've never seen mountains like this, so green with pines that last through all the seasons. It's strange to see such a big place so deserted. I keep expecting to see a kid riding a Big Wheel down the hallway out of the corner of my eye. Anyway, it must come to snow very early in the year, up this far."

"Which is all the more reason why you'll need this sweater!"

"Sophie, you know you can wear anything of mine that you like. I've never complained before."

"I do know that. Still, I've never really had a reason to feel so grand before. You saw that ballroom, and the dining parlor! I just thought it would be nice to dress up a little for a change."

"I never liked the outfit, anyway." Tess grabbed it in a quick motion and handed it to her friend without ceremony. She never asked her for much and if owning the dress as opposed to borrowing it was to her liking, she'd give her a dozen more if she could. The important thing was to make Sophie understand she wasn't imposing.

Besides, that cardigan was definitely going to come in handy. Tess took it gratefully when she handed it to her in exchange. Ryan was more than a little vague when they asked him how long it would be before they presented themselves to the directors at the company. He certainly had enough evidence in his files to prove who she was, but without the proper protocol papers, they had no real idea what might happen.

It all left Tess feeling sad, even lonely in a certain way. Here they were in the middle of nowhere, probably on another wild goose chase to find out more about her life, and even then Sophie was not lacking for company. *I'm lucky to have them both as my friends,* Tess thought to herself. Sophie wouldn't like Ryan if he wasn't a good man.

The phone rang sharply, causing the women to jump. She smiled, knowing what her own thoughts were, but could guess what her friend was daydreaming about as she pulled the soft fabric of her new dress through her fingers.

The voice on the other end of the line was perfectly polite and inquired after her comfort before he offered to light the fireplace in her suite of rooms. The evening was sure to become cool after sunset. She informed hospitality that they would be dining in the formal hall for the evening, and asked them to have a special bottle of champagne set out for the trio.

"Apparently my trust fund can afford this hotel," Tess laughed as she hung the receiver up onto the cradle. "We'll see how well when the bottle of wine comes. In the meantime, let's split apart and get ready for dinner. It will be fun to make a grand entrance into the dining hall, so dress up fancy."

Sophie needed no additional encouragement with her prize clutched in her hands and Tess was delighted to see the light in her eyes. She may have never known her own family, but Sophie was as much a sister as any she might have been born with.

Tess pulled a soft satin gown out of the garment bag, and the supple waves of emerald green cascaded to the floor as she held it up to her figure.

Sophie would be wearing a full dress to dinner, why shouldn't she? She hung the gown on a stand next to the vanity and noticed the white pamphlet peeking out over the pocket of her bag where she had hastily inserted it before they boarded.

With hesitation she reached inside to retrieve the program. She ran her fingers over the glossy cover with the delicately arced wings of the amphitheater in the forefront. Tess had never been to Sydney but her mind told her she had seen the opera house in person just days ago. She knew it was something she had to get over, put behind her so to speak, before she would be able to move on. After all, didn't she have enough on her plate without entertaining impossible fantasies?

"Still, that guy was one hot fantasy. Who could blame me?" she said to herself and laid the program on the table top. It really couldn't hurt to keep a piece of paper, could it?

When Tess had first encountered her mystery man she was embarrassed by the juvenile outfit she was caught wearing before he took her to the dance floor. Perhaps on this night, when she was in the company of her friends, it could be fun to dress as she wished she had been ... dressed for the opera on a warm and sultry evening in Australia.

Her black stockings were so sheer that you could barely tell there was a weave between her pale skin and their smooth casing. She believed that garters were far sexier than the elastic practicality of the mass-marketed brands, and she pressed the gossamer band of the old fashioned hose into the clasp that dangled on the end of the satin strip.

Tess slipped her feet into a daring pair of patent leather heels and knelt down to buckle the straps that accentuated her slender ankles. Though she had never worn the dress before, it was perfectly obvious her back would be exposed by the design. That was probably why she had never dared to wear the emerald beauty on any other occasion. Her nearly white skin was flawless, nothing she had ever been ashamed of previously, but she had also never been brave enough to bare so much of it in the past.

They were all adults now and it was time to do things she may have hesitated to do before, as a member of the student in the body of a large and prestigious university.

She stood bare-breasted in front the gilded mirror on the vanity, the cool air from her suite prickling her skin into goose bumps. Tess stepped into the gown and pulled the supple fabric over her hips before she finally tied the strap around her neck. Though the dress touched the floor at the tip of her toes, she felt completely exposed by the thin material that began to conform to her skin as her body heat softened the folds.

Tess ran hesitant hands over her figure, smoothing the dress against her curves as she dared to turn for a glimpse of her back in the mirror. The dress fell in perfect symmetry around her hourglass shape and she gathered her hair on top of her head with one last act of bravery.

The lush red lipstick was her final accessory and as she swept the wet, vibrant color across the delicate skin of her lips she shivered, remembering what his rough cheek had felt like against them just one week ago.

"I don't know about you," she addressed the glamorous stranger that was her own reflection in the mirror, "but I think I could really use a glass of that special wine right now."

Tucking her keycard into her satin purse, Tess left her room with one light on. After she was sure the lock clicked into place, she gathered the long skirt of her gown in her free hand and began to make her way down the corridor.

The lights seemed unusually dim and they even

flickered once or twice, but it was the silence all around that unnerved her. The carpet was very thick beneath her feet and the walls were covered with some type of noise reducing materiel. Several of the guest rooms had small halls of their own that went back into shadowy alcoves and she felt a little edgy when she passed those areas.

The strange smell near the end of the hall caused her to freeze in her tracks. It was sharp and acrid, reminding her of the way the air smells before an electrical storm ... It also reminded her of the way the air was in the alley the night her mysterious dance partner disappeared into nowhere.

The doorknob of the nearest guest room began to glow a very faint shade of orange and the sharp sound of sparks clearly came from the other side of the wood.

Tess's heart beat painfully in her chest and though she wanted to run toward the source of the familiar anomaly, her feet took her backward, slowly, into one of the shadowy alcoves she just passed. As much as she had fantasized about meeting the handsome stranger again, the hair on the back of her neck stood on end and she could not suppress the terrible feeling she had in the pit of her stomach.

She hung back as far as she could inside the recess without losing her view of the apartment across the hall. After the invasive sounds from the interior had ceased, a total silence fell in the corridor.

Just as she began to tell herself it had all been her imagination, the filigreed brass knob began to turn and the door opened with such silence it was unsettling. Had she been standing right next to the thing she never would have heard it.

Without realizing it, she had been holding her breath. A dark figure slunk with fluid motion through the open doorway. The moment Tess realized it was not her heart's desire two more silent partners joined the stalker in the corridor.

The suspended air in her lungs rushed from her lips with a tiny gasp. The sound didn't escape the attention of the newcomers. One of them turned his head in her direction.

Just as she decided to bolt down the corridor in the other direction a firm hand covered her mouth. A strong arm encircled her waist, pulling her back into the shadows as far as they could hide.

"I don't think I need to tell you how this goes, but just in case," his deep voice filled her ears with the smallest of whispers. "Do not make a sound. If they discover us, we'll both be in dire straits."

Four

He took his hand away from her lips the moment she nodded and he understood she remembered him. He slipped it into his pocket and pulled out a small, black plastic square that he stuck to the wall on their right. Tess was trembling despite her resolve to be strong, but she wasn't sure if it was due to her surprise at seeing him again or because of the intruders in the hallway.

He pressed a button on the exterior display of the tiny device and the air shimmered in front of them slightly before it settled down to normal. She barely dared to breathe as the shadows of the strangers grew in length along the wall of the main corridor. They became blacker and shorter as they neared the location where she had foolishly made the sound.

Tess lifted her chin and silently threaded her fingers through his large hand around her middle before she pulled them both down to her side. There was no doubt that they would have to run and she didn't want their limbs to be caught up in one another's when the time came. She just found him again and there was no way in hell she was going down without a fight.

Her dress would hinder her a little. She would have

regretted putting it on for the first time that night, if her magician had not been absentmindedly running his thumb up and down the silken seam along her hip.

Her heart thundered with such force that she was dizzy from the blood flow. She knew any second the intruders would peer around the corner and discover the two of them pressed together in the darkness.

The lead man came into view first and Tess nearly fell apart at the sight of him, though she knew it was coming. Her fingers were white with the pressure she put on her companion's hand and she was grateful for the fact that he was behind her for support as her frame pressed against him out of instinct.

Every muscle in her body strained to the snapping point and the image of breaking away to flee dominated her thoughts. As if he sensed this, her protector took his right hand and laid it gently against her exposed chest, where surely her heart was beating loud enough that the whole hotel could hear.

The darkly clad trio looked into the alcove where they hid, squinted slightly ... and moved on.

Tess's shoulders collapsed when they passed and she realized just how frightened she'd been. Still, she did not dare to move until she could be sure they were gone completely.

Her left hand remained inside his and his right palm kept its place over her heart. He might have been gauging her state after their close encounter, but after the immediate danger was over she was acutely aware of the way her entire body was pressed into him in a very intimate manner.

His chest was firm against her bare back. The heat from her exposed skin must be blazing through his clothing and at that thought her heart began to speed up again.

"They didn't see us," she whispered as quietly as she could. "How could they possibly have missed us from six feet away?"

"This small device on the wall is an invisibility cloak, to use a general term."

Tess could hear the smile in his voice as he spoke. She wondered if he was having her on because there was no such technology and he knew she wouldn't believe him. Still, with everything that had happened, who was she to discount anything? She was pretty close to believing the impossible at the moment.

"Alright then, Mr. Wizard, let's say that's true. How does it work?"

"It, um, doesn't make us invisible, as you can see." He gently pushed her forward a few inches and drew an involuntary breath at the full sight of her pale, naked back.

Tess turned to face him. There was no angle in which she could present herself that the gown did not show her figure off to a stunning advantage.

"The device bends light around an object, or objects. Many prototypes failed at this task in the past because the thing they were shielding cast a shadow in noticeable light. Either this one is past the prototype stage or we are in enough darkness that it didn't give us away."

"So, will it hurt me if I step through it?"

"Not if you keep a hold on my hand, Tesla."

He said it with such a straight face that she almost believed him. If she was ever going to find out more about him and believe in this bizarre reality she would have to do this. Her inquisitive nature demanded it.

It was now or never.

Tess backed away from him, though she allowed her fingers to remain in his grasp. Her plan was to walk just a few inches past the barrier and still be inside their private hall in the event of danger.

Though she had braced herself for an odd feeling as she crossed over, there was nothing. Not even a glimpse of her stranger whose hand she still grasped when she turned to look behind. Everything came rushing in at that moment. Tess finally understood this was for real and all the things she had experienced were true. She really had seen the Sydney opera house. She really had been invisible.

And she was holding the hand of the man who could do all of those things. It was time she found out what was going on and she had every intention of doing so as she came back to the other side.

Tess had a dozen questions on the tip of her tongue, but they flew right out of her head as soon as she stepped through and saw the copper cylinder with its flashing lights. He was leaving and by the grip on her hand, he intended on taking her with him.

"Wait! Please, listen for a second. Who are you?"

How could she convince him to help her if she didn't even know his name?

He stopped before he attached the whirling interface to the doorknob and smiled at her in a tender way. Somehow her question affected him.

"Well, I suppose I may as well tell you my name is Simon."

"Simon, my friends are back there. I'm not saying for a second that I don't want to go with you, but could we just get them first? I can't leave them. I can't leave Sophie behind, please."

She tried to keep the tears from her eyes but they welled up when she said her friend's name out loud. Damn, at the end of the day Simon could be God for all she knew and she still wouldn't go with him only to save herself.

"Is there any chance that your friends know more about what's going on than you do?"

"I can tell you that I don't know what's going on at all. Unless they found a clue in the dining room, they are way behind the learning curve on this one.

"Tesla, I know this is hard to understand but I risked a lot to come here and intervene on your behalf. It is very dangerous for me to be anywhere near these people. If your friends are innocent as you say, they have them already; just as they would have had you."

"How do you know all of this?"

She dropped his hand for the first time and her blood ran cold at the thought of his involvement.

"I am no friend of PT, I assure you," he frowned at the name. "I might even ask you the same question, Tesla. You are the one they seek."

"Well, I have no answers. I've never had any. The only thing I really ever had in my life that I could trust was Sophie. Everything that happens to her is my fault now, even if I'm not directly responsible. And start calling me Tess, for the love of God." Her voice was instantly filled with bitterness.

"Every fiber in my being screams for me to take you to safety, but I must honor your wishes if you are to ever honor mine. Just promise me, if it comes down to it, you will let me protect you without interference?"

"I promise." Tess said the words he wanted to hear,

but her heart knew the truth.

Simon retrieved the inconspicuous square from the wall where they lingered and deactivated the cylinder at her request. He would take her through the hotel to search for her friends, but if they discovered something amiss she agreed to follow his instructions after that.

Tess had a lot of unanswered questions, but Sophie was her first priority. In a way, Simon was right. He could turn the tables just as easily and ask her what her business was with PT. He probably would, eventually, but it said something about his character that he respected her feelings enough to address the issue of her friends first.

The silence on their end of the wing was stifling, and it seemed the harder she strained to hear any sound the heavier it became. Simon took the lead, though he insisted she keep her fingers hooked in the side pocket of his form fitting black slacks. Even from behind he was stunningly handsome, with his black hair curling along the nape of his neck and brushing against the deep blue weave of his cable knit sweater.

They came to a gently curving staircase, the polished oak rail glistening as it ran down the side to guide them to the first floor. The landing was laid out in dark grey tiles, with cascading fountains and lush greenery underneath an expanse of glass that made up the ceiling of the atrium. It was very dark outside and Tess noticed as she looked up that the lights from the fountains reflected off the dome like flickering stars in the sky.

It would have been enchanting if the muffled sounds of crying weren't filtering through to them from across the courtyard. Tess lost control and pulled ahead of Simon before he grabbed her wrist and motioned for her to be still.

He paused for a maddening amount of time, no doubt to see if the click of her heels on the tile had given them away, but the sound of distress in the distance only grew with each passing second.

She was grateful that he took her hand firmly in his, even if it was to keep her from running off again unexpectedly. His shoes gave off no sound as they made their way through the colorfully lit fountains and bubbling streams of the atrium. Tess found herself walking on the balls of her feet to keep her heels from touching down on the stone surface. Though her legs ached from the effort she kept it up until they reached the source of the crying.

A young woman sat on the flagstones near the entrance of the dining parlor, with her face in her hands as she sobbed uncontrollably. At first glance she appeared to be a guest, but then Tess noticed the dark tennis shoes on her feet and the torn panty hose on her legs that she had partially tucked beneath her.

It was a good bet that she was a server from the kitchen. Simon drew the same conclusion and he released her hand to kneel next to the young woman.

"You're safe now. Everything is going to be alright." His voice was soothing and full of compassion. At that moment, even Tess believed him as he reached out and gathered the distressed girl into his arms. When her tears subsided, he placed a gentle finger beneath her chin and lifted her mascara streaked face so he could look into her eyes.

Tess was impatient to press on, to find her friends, but she knew that if something did happen to them an eyewitness was their best chance to understand what it was. If they could get any information from her at all, they would have to do it now before the police arrived and took the young woman away.

"I was serving the wine." The woman's voice was rough from the tears and Tess leaned closer so she could hear.

"They were such a sweet young couple. He was so shy and she obviously doted on him. I don't know what they could have done to cause this."

"Do you remember their names? It's very important for you to tell us if you can."

"I don't know, but they were at the Pelham table. It was a celebration of some sort. I'm not sure what kind. They had a special bottle of wine sent up. That's why I was there."

The back of Tess's throat became tight and she blinked several times to keep her eyes clear while they learned more. She knew it was Ryan and Sophie now, but she had to maintain control. If she was going to help them at all she would have to hear everything the wine stewardess said.

"These three men came into the parlor while I was standing at the table. They made a beeline for us with no hesitation. Their clothes were dark, all black with no logos or anything on them. It was so weird."

"At first they called the girl Tess, but she laughed and said they were mistaken. One of them grabbed her by the arm and asked where Tess was. That was when the shy fellow jumped up and pulled him off her. I dropped the wine. Oh my God, I have never dropped a bottle of wine in my life."

The serving girl was past her initial reaction to the assault and was obviously slipping into the later stages of shock. Her face took on a blank stare and her voice continued in a strangely surreal monotone.

"The bottle didn't break. I grabbed it and hit one of them over the head when he picked the girl up. It glanced off his skull. He pushed me into the table and they forced the young couple out of the room. I tried to follow them, but when I opened the door to the pantry they were gone."

Simon gently leaned her up against the planter and regained his feet. The girl stared into space, her hands limp in her lap. Tess noticed flashing lights against the dome now, red and blue and white. She knew they didn't have much time. The police were there and she couldn't help but wonder what would happen if the authorities decided to question Simon.

She looked up into Simon's eyes and realized he was thinking the same. With a swift but gentle motion he laid his hand on the traumatized girl's shoulder.

"Thank you for responding so quickly to my call, detective," She spoke to him with a faraway look in her eyes. "I just can't believe the bottle didn't break."

Of course, she thought Simon was a police officer.

Tess knew they had to get moving, and quickly, before the real detectives arrived on the scene.

"You did a fine job here tonight," he said with compassion. "Just leave the rest to us now."

They had a few precious moments before the place would be swarming with people who were going to want to ask Tess a lot of questions. Simon took her hand firmly and led her away from the serving girl to draw his conclusions.

"She said they entered the pantry, but when she opened the door they were gone."

Simon went through the grand double doors and into the dining hall where the incident took place. Signs of a struggle were everywhere, beginning at the table where Sophie and Ryan were waiting to dine and radiating along an obvious trail toward the kitchen. At least one of her friends had fought back on the way, which gave her a little hope as to the state of their well being.

"Do you think she'll be alright back there, until help comes?" Tess was still concerned for the brave girl's welfare and the fact that they left her alone, sitting up against a planter in the foyer.

"Help is at the door now and I guarantee you that the bad guys are long gone. We need to get to the pantry and make sure my suspicions are correct while we still have a chance."

"Do you suppose the trio who abducted my friends used a copper colored cylinder to open a door that led to some place other than the pantry for a late night snack?" If Simon noticed the frown on her face as she glanced at his pocket, he didn't acknowledge it.

The kitchen was deserted. They quietly threaded their way down the aisles, crowded with appliances and stainless steel shelves. She strained to listen for anything at all, but aside from a pot boiling on one of the stoves there was nothing.

Simon turned to face her when it was obvious they were alone. "You are very observant for a woman who doesn't know what's going on."

For just an instant she thought he was going to tell her something else, perhaps reveal more about his secret mode of travel. He must have thought better of it, because he turned back to the pantry instead.

Chicken, she thought to herself. If you can't even tell

me about this, what will I ever be able to know about you?

The door was closed, and Simon reached out to touch the old fashioned brass knob with his fingertips. Tess didn't need him to tell her it was still warm to the touch. She could still see, in her mind's eye, the red mark on the palm of the wine stewardess's hand as it lay in her lap.

He pulled the heavy door open all the way and she saw that every item inside was perfectly shelved and cataloged, as if nothing had touched the interior of the space. It was quite a contrast to the chaos and disorder all around them in the rest of the kitchen.

There was a shout in the corridor, causing Tess to jump. Simon pulled his own copper device from beneath his sweater and began to click the dial rapidly.

"Can this thing take us to the last place they went?" Tess looked nervously over her shoulder as the sounds of advancing footsteps grew more prominent.

"It can't recall where they have gone, but it's okay, I have a pretty good idea where they took your friends. After all, it's where you were trying to go all along."

"Are you suggesting those characters were from Poly Tech?" Tess's voice spiked in panic and she had to force herself to calm down.

"I am not suggesting it in any way. I'm telling you for certain."

"You have one of those ... things." She gestured at the sparking dial that he was attaching to the knob. "Those men had one as well. You are from Poly Tech too!"

"I'm not, Tess. I promise you. At least not anymore."

He completed the sequence and opened the door. It was dark past the threshold and a deep aroma of ancient, musty wood assaulted her senses when he stepped inside. Simon turned to offer his hand for the crossing.

"Not anymore means you once were." Tess hesitated at his offer, her heart telling her to step forward but her mind telling her to step back. He was clearly involved in some way, even admitted as much though he did not have the time to elaborate. Tess realized it would be more than foolish to go with him until she had more answers. A part of her wanted to selfishly fling herself into his arms and slam the door behind them forever, but the other half of her sensibilities reminded her that Sophie and Ryan were depending on her. She wouldn't be risking her own life if she laid her fate in Simon's hands, she'd be risking her friends as well.

"Miss, are you okay? Please, answer me!"

The police had obviously seen her, but they had not been in a position to view Simon's face through the opening in the door. They wouldn't enter the room all the way until they could ascertain the situation.

"I don't know," she answered out loud, but her words were meant for the man in the cable knit sweater on the other side of the doorway.

A look of panic crossed Simon's face, but he only mouthed one word.

Please.

Tess reached out a slender arm in his direction and gently closed the door until she heard the lock click into place. Then she turned to face the people who came to save her.

Five

The cabin was nearly pitch black inside. It didn't hinder Simon's movement, however. He often spent days at the retreat, hidden deep in the rugged mountains. It was the closest doorway to Poly Tech Acquisitions that he'd discovered to date, though nothing he tried had ever taken him inside the mountain facility itself.

He felt his way through the room with a practiced hand until he came to the cabinet filled with emergency gear in the small cooking area. It would have been easier to leave the flashlights out on the counter, but he always put everything back exactly the way he found it when he left.

A quick look around let him know that nothing was out of place since his last visit. Simon sat on the small couch near the cold fireplace with a heavy sigh. Technically, he didn't have a home to call his own. This was the closest thing since the accident, the only place he could return to without worry. It must have been omitted somehow from the official list of doorways the cylinder could slice, and a good thing too, because he didn't have that list. Probably wasn't even supposed to have the cylinder. He always assumed it was purely by chance that he dialed this location, though now he wondered just how much chance really had to do with his circumstances at all.

They said he had amnesia at the hospital, and he was forced to agree with them. But he could remember some things—things he suspected they would never believe if he told them. Before the medication wore off, he raved for a while about secret prototypes and spy-like technologies. All those confessions were greeted with sympathetic smiles from the nursing staff and a conciliatory pat on the shoulder.

He knew he was in trouble when the therapist began to come to his room on a regular basis. Phrases like "break from reality" and "a possible danger" were bandied about from around the corner where they thought he couldn't hear.

And so he left.

Simon quickly discovered that his memories were valid. The first time, they brought him to a small loft, tucked away among rusting warehouses with cracked, frosted glass windows. He found a lock box at that place, and his fingers flipped through the combination before he could fear he couldn't recall it. There was money in the box, a lot of it—and a copper cylinder.

No identification, however. He followed numerous clues from his memory and discovered a dozen caches like the first, but never anything with his name on it. Simon smiled when he remembered that Tess asked his name. He almost didn't know how to answer. He told her the first thing that came into his mind, one of his few intact memories that consisted of two young children playing a game together.

"I didn't say Simon Says!" The red-haired girl giggled

in this vibrant flash, pointing a finger at him. It was the only thing he kept close to his heart that felt good and real after everything he'd been through.

Simon felt more strongly than ever that Tess couldn't be a part of some insidious plot or nefarious behavior by the agency. Her fear for her friends was real. If only she had followed his instructions, he could be sure she'd be safe right now. It was eating him up inside, not knowing what was happening to her.

What drew him closer to the edge, though, was the fact he wanted to protect her. He had been so focused on his own life that no one had ever broken through that wall he kept around himself. One dance with Tesla and his barriers were crumbling down all over the place. It almost killed him to let her go at the hotel, but he knew if she was ever going to trust him he had to let her make her own choices. And he needed that, because she was the key to his past. As for his future—he didn't dare to hope that far ahead.

All he had was now and he only knew one thing: He had to find her again.

•

"I've told you a thousand times who I am and what I'm doing here. You have my identification and there can be no doubt that you've searched all of our suites by now. You're supposed to be helping me, remember?"

Tess was trying to keep her temper under wraps, but she had outlined her story so many times to so many detectives, that she was beginning to lose it. She never mentioned Simon once and maybe they sensed she was leaving something out, but nothing they did convinced her to give him away. Whatever he was doing at the hotel, it wasn't snatching her friends because he'd been with her the entire time. He could have forced her through the pantry door, yet he hadn't. Something in her heart told her she should keep him a secret. At least until she understood more about their situation.

Tess slammed her palms down on the polished Formica table. She rose a few feet to loom over the unfortunate officer currently assigned to verify her version of the events.

"I want to know where my friends are and what you're doing to recover them. How about that? Because if you're wasting your time with me you aren't looking for them, or following any other leads. I'm not stupid."

The door to the small room opened and Tess relished a moment of cool, fresh air. She wondered if they intentionally kept it hot inside the small space, just another tactic to make people uncomfortable enough to talk.

"You don't have to answer any more questions, Ms. Pelham," a new voice said through the doorway. A man moved past the attending officers like they were an offensive set of objects in his way, and at the same time he took the interrogator's chair by the back and placed it next to her at the table like he had every right to sit in it.

"I hope you all realize the grave mistake you have made this evening," the elderly man stated coolly as he hefted a large, black leather briefcase onto the table. "You may call me Doctor Greenfield, and I believe you are familiar with this young lady by now. Tesla Pelham is most certainly the heir apparent to Poly Tech Acquisitions, as I'm sure she must have told you. Mr. Laconia has verified that information himself and it does not distress me at all to inform you that he is very displeased with her treatment."

"Mr. Laconia sent you?" The lead officer on her case backed into the nearest corner and looked at both of them as if they were either famous or dangerous. Tess wasn't sure which it was, but she felt a small measure of satisfaction now that the tables were turned. The officer who spent the last half hour insinuating her guilt was obviously engaged in an epic struggle to repress the look of horror on his face.

"Oh, he did much more than that. In fact, he is waiting outside in a secured vehicle to escort the young lady back to our facilities himself."

The shattering sound of glass just outside the room caused the detective to jump nervously away from his post. It was just as well because the heavy metal door flew open again a moment later.

"Mr. Laconia came down off the mountain?"

The newcomer was a pudgy, older gentleman with coffee stains on his shiny shoes. He was red in the face, and he clutched his hands together until his knuckles were white. It was apparent to everyone there that he was working up his nerve to speak again.

"Do you think I might ask him a few questions? There are a couple of things I need to be clear on, not just events from tonight either, and he so rarely makes an appearance anywhere near the town—"

"He is always happy to assist the local authorities, Sergeant Martin. I believe he anticipated your request and has instructed the head of his security detail to await you in your office at precisely this moment."

"I was hoping I could see him in person, you understand. I have never really met him and it has been so long since anyone has actually seen him, now that I think about it."

"I'm sure he will be delighted to socialize with you once this whole kidnapping business is straightened out. He is gravely concerned for the well being of these youngsters who have gone missing and has assigned Mr. Chelsith to assist you directly until the matter is resolved. I'm sure he is making himself quite at home at your desk as we speak."

"Mr. Chelsith is in my office right now ... by himself?"

"I believe he is, as I said a minute ago."

Sergeant Martin straightened up immediately. He ran a nervous hand through his grey hair before he used it to slap the nearby detective on the back of his head.

"What are you doing Justin? Release poor Ms. Pelham into Laconia's custody already! Hasn't she been through enough for one evening?"

•

It had been so hot in that building that Tess didn't realize she was still scantily dressed in her evening gown until she stepped outside and into the night air of the Colorado mountains.

The soft skin of her forehead was moist from the uncomfortable room and the icy wind struck her like a cold slap in the face. The moment she hesitated, Dr. Greenfield paused and looked at her with genuine concern.

"If you'd like to take a moment to compose yourself before meeting Mr. Laconia, it is understandable of course."

"He's really out there, sitting in a car, waiting for me? Are we going to his secret underground lair?"

As she spoke, Tess had visions of a bald villain with one monocle attached to his right eye, glaring as he manically stroked a white cat with a diamond collar.

"Nothing so cliché, I assure you my dear, though I must admit that our facility is located partially inside the face of a mountain to the north."

"Tell me the truth, Dr. Greenfield. Is it going to be safe there? It's hard for me to know who to trust after everything that happened this evening. The police didn't exactly afford me all the help I'd hoped for when I went with them tonight, either."

"If you're going to ask me so many questions, I think I'd like for you to call me by my first name, which is Alan." He walked around her in a complete circle, whistling low when he completed his observation.

"I'll be honest with you, young miss. I know Mr. Laconia to be totally trustworthy with issues of business and camaraderie. I daresay, though, you might be in no small amount of danger clothed in that enchanting gown on a chilly evening."

"Oh!" Tess wrapped her arms across her chest and gripped her shoulders with the palms of her hands. The last thing she wanted in this situation was to reveal anything that could make her vulnerable in front of some eccentric, power hungry old goat in the back of his car.

"Might I offer you my smoking jacket? You can be assured that I don't smoke anything more than a pipe by the fire, on occasion." The doctor set his case on the ground and swung the deep green velvet coat from his shoulders with ease before he held it out to her.

Tess gratefully accepted his gift and when he picked up his case to continue down the drive she walked with him willingly. It was dark very early, this deep in the hills. She would have missed the black sedan if it hadn't been for the muted yellow lights on the vehicle that indicated it was parking.

The engine was so quiet when they approached she wasn't sure if the car was running until they got close enough for her to see a slight stream of mist coming from the tailpipe. The windows were tinted as black as the night sky, which only served to remind her that once she was behind the glass she was as good as invisible to everyone in the outside world.

Invisible. Tess thought back to an earlier point in time when Simon had sheltered her with a miracle. Though she promised him she would follow his instructions, she had not done so. She reminded herself once more that her friends were at stake and the police seemed like the most trustworthy option at that moment, even if they didn't come through at the end.

Though she liked Dr. Greenfield right off the bat, she couldn't help but wonder if she was any better off than she might have been if she had left all of their fates in Simon's hands. As it stood now, she was about to get into a car with some old man whose intentions were completely unknown.

Still, this was as close as she had ever gotten to anything that had something to do with her parents. This place is where they wanted her to be. She knew they must have had history with some of the people there. This was the last thing they willed to her and she was dragging her feet like an uncertain child. All those years of schooling and culture meant they wanted her to become who she was now and she had to be ready. That final thought was more than enough to encourage her to walk right up to the door and set her fingers on the chrome handle.

"Allow me, Tesla." Dr Greenfield spoke her proper

name fondly and for once she did not despise it as it rolled off his tongue.

Her newfound friend gracefully opened the door with his right hand and gestured magnanimously inside to the gentleman seated within.

"Tesla Pelham, may I introduce you to Emory Laconia?"

It turned out to be quite lucky that she had removed her hand from the cold, silver handle on the car door. She needed it now to cover her mouth as she came face to face with the head of Poly Tech Acquisitions.

Six

She was stunned, unable to move or speak. The dark-haired man inside the car turned to Dr. Greenfield with an inquisitive smile before he faced her.

"Although I'd like to think I exceed the expectations of those who meet me for the first time, I don't usually have quite this effect on the young ladies, Alan."

He looked at her with Simon's face—spoke to them with Simon's lips!

Tess could barely breathe as her gaze fell on his beautiful, deep blue eyes. She nearly blurted out his name, giving herself away before she realized that there was no recognition of her in those familiar orbs.

Curiosity was there, sure. But this man in front of her had never seen her before this evening and though she couldn't find any way to prove it wasn't just an act, she could feel it deep down inside her soul.

The person seated in the car was identical to Simon in every way. Well, that wasn't exactly true, because Tess understood the fact that he simply wasn't the man she met on that extraordinary evening in London when she lost her heart on the dance floor. She couldn't explain it, but she didn't feel that bond, that passion that curled up inside her soul and waited to be near him again.

Emory Laconia was a stranger. And he was a stranger who was beginning to develop a look of concern on his face at her obvious confusion and hesitation. Of course her behavior would seem out of the ordinary, even in their current situation. She certainly hadn't reacted to Dr. Greenfield in such a manner, and if she didn't manage to pull herself together immediately, she was going to give something away.

"Mr. Laconia, thank you so much for helping me tonight. I'm not sure what I would have done if you hadn't discovered I was being held in the local lock up for heaven only knows what."

He smiled in response to her statement of gratitude and visibly relaxed. When he motioned for her to join him inside the car, Dr. Greenfield held her hand and guided her gently onto the warm, leather seats. Tess had stoically resolved to keep her guard up next to the stranger, but as the supple leather conformed to her back and neck, she closed her eyes momentarily to lean into the comforting heat.

"Would you like to ride up the mountain with us, Alan?" Mr. Laconia asked the doctor who lingered near the open door with a watchful eye on Tess.

"It is very kind of you to offer, but sadly enough my car won't drive itself back. I don't think you've managed to invent that little treasure yet, have you?"

"I assure you I've got people working on it, my friend." Mr. Laconia laughed pleasantly and the sound of it was natural enough that she imagined their friendship was probably genuine, though what the kind elderly gentleman could have in common with the young CEO was beyond her.

Tess was more confused than ever. Now that she was alone with the man who held the legacy of her parents in his hands, she found all the questions she'd been saving up for a lifetime slip away. Her situation was nothing like she imagined it would be.

The car pulled onto the road and she found herself pressed into the soothing bucket seats as the sedan gracefully navigated a steep hill. The windows were so black she couldn't see a thing outside, and the tinted divider between her host and the driver only served to remind her of how isolated she was now. They might as well blindfold her, for all that she'd be able to recall about the route they were taking.

"Please, Ms. Pelham. I know your feelings toward me might not be warm at the moment, but I hope you will forgive me for the events that have occurred this evening. I can't help but feel responsible for what happened to your friends."

Tess immediately thought back to what Simon said to her at the pantry door. He was sure that the thugs who abducted Sophie were from Poly Tech Acquisitions. Was this man confessing the truth to her now that he had her at his mercy? If that was the case, did he know about Simon as well?

"How should I feel about you, Mr. Laconia? If you know something I do not, I'd appreciate it if you would fill me in so I'm not completely in the dark."

He sighed and favored her with a strange smile that made her more than a little uncomfortable in its intensity.

"When I recently discovered that Kurt and Anna's daughter had survived, I was just breathless with the hope that it could be true. Ryan approached security as soon as you all arrived, but he did not do it through the proper channels. I'm afraid that is how all of this started and if I had just believed him from the start we might have prevented the calamity that occurred. I never should have turned him away."

Tess pulled the velvet jacket closer across her chest when she realized her companion had turned in his seat, holding her gaze with an overpowering stare. He was searching for something in her eyes, maybe some kind of reaction that would confirm her belief in his story.

"Don't you remember me, my dear Tess? I recall how we played together as children. You are more beautiful now than my memory could ever have grown you. I can hardly believe we are together again."

His lips parted and he leaned slightly forward as he reached out to gently touch her cheek. Tess was silent, unable to react to his gesture as glimpses of the past flashed through her mind. It was a game they played, on the lawn while their parents worked ... Oh my God, she did remember him!

His eyes were locked onto hers, but he didn't see her. He was viewing another time and place as well. She had to stop him right away, before anything happened that moved this evening from bad to worse.

"Mr. Laconia, we were just talking about my friends. Do you have any idea where they are right now?"

He slid his palm away from her cheek when the mood was broken and patted her hand before he turned back in his seat. Whatever ardor had inspired his advance evaporated and he seemed quite the gentleman again.

"You're right, of course. What was I thinking? We've

had some issues at the facility in recent years, I'm sorry to say. It has forced us to shore up our security measures to protect the various projects we are contracted to complete. The access protocols are there for a reason, you see. I'm sure when Ryan did not approach by the proper channels his actions alerted certain necessary security squads who would need to ask him a few questions."

"I don't care about anything right now except for the safety of my friends, Mr. Laconia. If you can help me at all, please help me. If I really am a part of this company now, or whatever it is, I want you to call off the dogs right now."

"Don't worry for them, Tess. I expect their safe return at any moment. May I still call you Tess?"

She disregarded his question. The last thing she was concerned about at the moment was the way in which he addressed her.

"How can you know that? How do you know they'll return unharmed?"

"It usually happens that way, my dear. Just leave everything to me."

"Usually? I don't find that reassuring, you should know." Tess wasn't certain if she should be suspicious of her new host, but she was on the train heading there and it didn't look like anyone was going to be hitting the brakes anytime soon.

Though Mr. Laconia had removed his hand from her face earlier, she noticed he had taken up a piece of her gown that had crossed over to his side of the car. With absentminded strokes he ran his thumb and forefinger along the seam in almost the same manner Simon had done in the corridor of the hotel.

The parallel was astonishing and she silently prayed that they would arrive at their destination soon. Tess was exhausted and she needed time alone to think about all the information she had received since they came to the resort. She didn't want to sleep, though, far from it. How could she rest when her friends were out there, possibly struggling to survive?

The sedan slowed and the feel of the pavement beneath them changed as they entered a tunnel. Tess recalled what Dr. Greenfield had said earlier, about the facility being partially inside a mountain. If that was true, and it seemed to be, she would never get past security if she needed to. It was hard to tell what she was going to need at that point though, and the bottom line was that she was where she was supposed to be. She inherited Poly Tech Acquisitions, some of it at least, and for the first time in her life she belonged.

Tess could only hope that she didn't belong to a secret society that cloned evil dictators in Brazil or something.

She couldn't let herself be intimidated by anyone in this place, no matter what happened. She was new to the facility, but she was a smart girl and had a right to be there. Tess had every intention of taking over the reins someday.

The car stopped and only a few seconds lapsed before her door opened to reveal a plainly dressed fellow with rather large biceps who offered his hand to help her out. She wondered if he was part of the new security for the compound. After all, she had never seen a driver who could bench press a Bentley before.

They were in a cavernous underground parking garage and every sound her heels made on the smooth cement echoed for a mile. The driver held onto her hand a little longer than necessary as the voluminous skirts of her gown spread out and caressed the floor of the garage with a delicate whisper.

"Rafe, if you could just get Ms. Pelham's things and take them to her room, I'm sure she'd like to change and get settled in before we go any further."

The muscular man quickly dropped her hand and looked at his shoes as he walked over to the trunk of the black sedan. Her personal items were visible inside the back of the car and she turned to Mr. Laconia with a suspicious look.

"Did you go into my room? Did you go through my things?" Tess instantly panicked, thinking only of the Sydney Opera program, though it shouldn't incriminate her in any way.

"Of course not. The local authorities procured your items before I arrived at the station. I merely requested that they transfer your belongings to me so that I could make you as comfortable as possible while you are my guest."

He appeared to be taken aback by her accusation and she couldn't help but mentally kick herself for her outburst. She was very tired and her circumstances were bizarre at best, but behaving badly would not get her off to a good a start.

She wasn't a guest, though. This was her life now and she'd be damned if she needed an invitation to visit it. As Emory escorted her through the garage she got the distinct feeling that Dr. Greenfield's refined velvet smoking jacket had a great big target on the back.

Seven

"We do have extended sleeping quarters at the facility," Emory explained as they left the open space in the garage and entered softly lit corridors. The contrast of environments was a little disorienting, every sound now muted as they walked along. "Our staff will often do what we refer to as 'tours' when they work on special projects. Their focus must be committed twenty-four-hours a day for crucial work. These employees have what could really be termed as a second home here."

Tess already imagined what the accommodations would be like. Everything she'd seen so far had military overtones to it—from the security to the vehicles in the garage. She was surprised when the austere décor gave way to a comfortable, if not elegant, home setting.

Along the wall, curtains hung over windows that couldn't serve a function if they were really underground. She had to refrain from going over to pull them back and see. Family portraits hung alongside the rich fabric drapes, pictures of the staff and their relatives, no doubt.

She briefly wondered if this setup had been her parents' idea. She liked to think they would have cared so much about their employees that they would have done anything to make them happy. She even had a few early memories of time at the facility as a young child. With the tightened security precautions, however, much of that family atmosphere might have been sacrificed.

She felt like she was in a grand plantation house as they climbed the large staircase to the second floor and stopped in front of a door near the landing. Tess was relieved when Emory handed her a key card and she saw the hotel-like locking system beneath the handle. She thought that perhaps, in a place of absolute security, there wouldn't be locks and was glad that wasn't the case.

She repressed a smile when she saw Security Level One typed boldly above the magnetic strip on the card. She was going to need a lot more than that when she was ready. The lock clicked smoothly when she placed the key in the slot. As Emory moved to open the door for her his mobile phone vibrated and he stepped back into the hall to answer it.

"I see. And it was successful?" His tone was nonchalant, but she could see the tight edges around his lips as he spoke. "You're completely sure? I'm glad to hear it. Will you join us for dinner, then?"

Tess wanted to hear his conversation almost more than anything in the world at the moment, but it was too obvious for her to hover nearby so she reluctantly entered the room.

To say it was a room was an understatement. A full suite greeted her, larger than most of the apartments she had stayed in during her college years. The furnishings were beautiful and comfortable looking at the same time. Her luggage was already inside, though thankfully it wasn't unpacked.

If anyone had to spend a great deal of time at the facility, they wouldn't be put out while doing so.

Sophie would love this place, Tess thought and her mind focused on the reality of her situation again. This wasn't a vacation and she had to quit acting like it. She really wanted to get out of the evening gown, but was stuck until the stranger in the hall decided to take his leave. Fortunately for her, the call was short. He rapped politely on the open door, but didn't wait for an answer before he entered.

"Is everything alright? Was that call about Sophie and Ryan?" She pulled the doctor's jacket tightly around her figure in case Emory Laconia got any more amorous ideas.

"It was, actually. Turns out they've been clearing security all this time and my staff is just getting back to me about it. You'd think with all our fabulous technology we'd have a handle on timely communication, eh?"

"They've been here all evening and you didn't know? How could you not know what's going on at your own company, Mr. Laconia?" Tess tried to keep her voice down, but she was practically shouting at the end. She knew it wasn't polite, but she was pissed.

"Miss Pelham, you have my sincerest apologies. Please allow me remind you that I had to leave the mountain for another urgent matter. Once outside the domain of the facility, contact is strictly limited."

Well, he had her there. Of course he meant his retrieval of her person at the sheriff's station. While she was glad he hadn't left her there to suffer, she still didn't like his excuse any better.

"I want to see them right now." Tess crossed the

room and stood face to face with Mr. Laconia. She fully expected him deny her request and prepared herself for battle.

She was so close to him that she could feel his breath on her skin as she looked into his eyes with waiting defiance.

"My God, Tess," he whispered, his eyes wide and glossy. "You are incredibly beautiful when you're angry."

She could hardly believe his reaction to her threatening stance and took a few steps back before crossing her arms over her chest. His behavior was just too much to comprehend, especially given their circumstances. It was almost like he was inexperienced with controlling his emotions and interacting with her on a social level.

"So, are you taking me to see them?" She was at his mercy whether she liked it or not, so she would try to be civil.

"I thought you might want to change first, of course. Mr. Chelsith mentioned your friends were hungry when we spoke, so I thought we'd have dinner despite the late hour."

Tess longed to get out of her dress and the news that Sophie was requesting dinner went a long way toward making her feel better. She could do with a bite herself, in fact.

"If you would tell me where the dining room is, I think I can find my way when I'm ready." She had no intention of letting him wait anywhere nearby as she changed. He looked disappointed, but nodded his agreement.

"Go down the main stairs we just ascended. When you get to the bottom, walk back through the corridor behind them. You'll find us through the kitchen, on the patio. And Tess, don't wander outside of the living area. There are many experiments taking place throughout the facility and it's not safe without the proper clearance."

Tess was already walking him to her door and she wasn't surprised by his warning as she closed it. She'd seen enough episodes of "Eureka" on the SyFy channel to understand how dangerous secret military projects could be, but she doubted that was his only reason for keeping her tethered. He didn't have to worry, however—at least not at the moment. Her first concern was to see to the safety of her friends and if they were on the patio, that's where she'd be too.

•

Simon was nervous. Anyone who had just stolen a police uniform from the laundry hamper in the locker room of the precinct would be. The uniform smelled a little bit like licorice and root beer, too. It could have been a lot worse.

He first thought the police force in the small town was massive, until he noticed an eclectic collection of uniforms and county squad cars. They must have marshaled the forces from the surrounding jurisdictions for the emergency. All this actually made his job a lot easier. He wandered inconspicuously through the crowd, grabbing a piece of a uniform here, an insignia pin there. By the time his costume was complete it consisted of so many different parts that no one thought him out of place in any one of them.

Exposing himself so openly, and this close to the facility, was a risk Simon had never taken before. The heat was on Tess and her friends for the moment, but it didn't make him feel any better. Whoever ran the show inside Poly Tech Acquisitions had his hands full, he was sure of that. It was a freedom Simon had never known before. And it meant that Tess was even more important, or in more danger, than he had guessed.

He had to make sure she wasn't in trouble, locked away in a cell somewhere and being mistreated. He knew these guys meant business, but she didn't. It was true that he couldn't remember what went on inside the compound, or even what it had to do with him. But he was driven by a powerful need to get inside. And if he could do that, maybe his life would come back to him.

Was he a spy? A thief? How did he come into possession of all those mysterious items if he wasn't? He wondered what Tess would think of him then. It didn't matter anyway—it was useless to guess at the truth. All he could be was what he was today.

He reached inside his inner jacket pocket and took out a pair of sunglasses. It had taken him a long time to get used to them at first, and he found that if he wore them for any extended period his head throbbed afterward. He almost tossed them when he came across them in Oslo, along with the pile of cash he thought was more valuable at the time. Fortunately the sun was bright that day and he'd just come from the other side of the globe where it'd been dark.

He soon discovered that he could see things with them—metal things. It didn't matter what they were encased in or what covered them up. He could make out computer chips inside cell phones and see the fillings inside people's teeth. The glasses had come in handy on more than one occasion when he had to determine who had the gun and who didn't. He hoped he wouldn't have to keep them on long tonight. There was no time for a debilitating headache when he had so much to do.

Simon scanned the area and found what he was looking for right away. Two police officers lounged against the side of the precinct having a smoke. They were far enough away they wouldn't be noticed, but close enough they could come running if called. These men were stationed inside.

The heavier of the two leaned forward and coughed. Simon could see the pacemaker through his chest and frowned. Cigarettes weren't such a good idea for this guy, and by the way he was hiding he knew it. It was show time.

Simon slipped the glasses off and strolled casually toward the errant officers. When he got close he held out his hand and offered the ailing fellow a wide smile.

"Hey there, my man. How's the old ticker doing?"

"Do I know you?" The heavyset man's eyes narrowed, but he still shook Simon's hand reluctantly.

"Do I know you, you mean? Has the Captain heard you started smoking again? 'Cause I don't think I want to know you when he finds out." Simon laughed and took a step back, holding up his hands in defense.

"Oh hell. You're not gonna tell him, are you? You have to understand, it's all the stress. They said Emory Laconia came down off the mountain tonight, and I ain't ever seen him before. No one has, man. I was scared, like maybe there was some kind of meltdown up there or something. Turns out it was just some broad that tried to break into his headquarters."

"She still inside the precinct?" Simon kept his tone casual, but mention of Emory Laconia's name sent his heart hammering in his chest. He'd heard it before, of course, but something about it sent his senses into a tailspin every time.

"No way, they escorted her up the mountain hours ago. In a limo, too. How's that for some fancy treatment after breaking and entering? Anyway, the rest of their snooty private security detail is being recalled, so they'll be gone soon and we can all relax down here."

She was already at the facility. *Damn.* His head was spinning with ideas, but nothing he could grab on to. He needed to get close to the departing caravan. Maybe he could pick up some information that might help him find a way inside.

"I'll be looking forward to getting out of here, myself." Simon offered his hand to the officer again and this time the man shook it heartily.

"Hey, you're not going to say anything about this, right? The smoking, I mean. I'm not going to make it a habit."

"Not a word, but if you don't quit for good it won't matter." Simon nodded and released the handshake.

He blended back into the crowd with no trouble, dropping pieces of his uniform along the way to the last line of unmarked security cars. These sedans were top of the line, black with tinted windows all the way around. Even more impressive was the private security staff, also dressed in black and armed to the teeth. Unfortunately, he soon realized he wasn't going to overhear any idle chatter or gossip from this bunch.

Simon did a quick check to make sure he'd removed anything shiny from his clothing. Once satisfied, he reached into his pants pocket to pull out the cloaking device he'd come to rely on heavily the past few days. It was the only thing that could get him close enough to gather information.

He held the tiny button on the surface of the smooth square down until the green light came on. He'd have to move slowly, and even then there would be a trace of his form, almost ghost-like to the naked eye. It seemed to work best when he was completely still.

So, his brilliant plan was this: crawl into the back of one of the open sedans and sit as still as possible while looking and listening for information. It was working, too. No one noticed him as he silently climbed inside and sat on one of the leather seats.

There was a plain, black book securely tucked into the back pocket behind one of the seats. He'd have to reach for it and get it inside the field of his cloaking device. It was set to a very narrow radius, just enough to cover him.

Just as his fingers closed around the binder he heard a clicking noise and realized with horror that the sound was coming from him.

"What is that?" A voice from the exterior of the car hissed in a barely audible tone. Simon glanced at the tiny device in his left hand and saw the green light was blinking. Was it running out of power? It was true that he'd never used it as much as he had recently, but he couldn't remember a way to charge it.

The sound of crunching gravel surrounded the vehicle and the moment the silence fell the green light went out altogether. He was completely exposed.

"Let me see your hands!" A rough voice barked through the open door, allowing his firearm to lead the way into the back of the car. Simon couldn't move, his muscles frozen by the realization that he'd finally been caught.

The burly man, dressed in Poly Tech black, leaned all

the way inside. Simon expected the worst, but defiantly made eye contact with the aggressor. He wasn't the type to go down without a fight. Before he could rise to the occasion, the security agent's eyes grew wide and he promptly sheathed his gun.

"I apologize, sir. I didn't recognize you." His face was a mask of nervous concern. "The last of the men are ready to depart now. I take full credit for the delay, but as you can see now, everything is in order. Will you be traveling up the mountain with us, Mr. Laconia?"

EIGHT

Tess could hear voices as she walked down the corridor and into the kitchen. It sounded like normal, happy chatter. She was feeling much better herself, dressed in a pair of comfortable slacks with Sophie's sweater buttoned up over her T-shirt. The kitchen looked a lot like the one back at the resort, and just as large.

The lingering aroma of food made her mouth water and she realized it had been a while since she'd eaten anything. She pushed through one of the doors on the other side of the tiled room and came out onto a veranda of sorts. Still underground, it was encased in a greenhouse with a small yard and warm lights placed above the glass.

"Ah, glad you could join us on the porch for a little dinner, Ms. Pelham." Emory Laconia smiled as he rose from his place behind a country table. He seemed very formal and stiff after his familiarity earlier, but she didn't have time to wonder about it. Ryan sprang up from his chair, toppling it over as he rushed to her side.

"Oh my God, are you okay? We have been so worried about you." He put his hand on her shoulder and searched her face for a response. Tess assumed that by "we" he meant Sophie and himself, but she noticed out of the corner of her eye that her best friend had remained seated, and very close to Mr. Laconia at that. She wondered if Sophie would recognize the head of Poly Tech Acquisitions from her brief contact with Simon at the night club. To Tess, the two men appeared to be identical.

"Me? After they abducted you from the hotel I thought I'd never see you again. I was scared to death." She pulled away from Ryan's hold and turned in Sophie's direction, but she didn't notice Tess at all.

"What do you mean, abducted?" Her friend laughed a little nervously, confused by the response. "We were just waiting for you at dinner and the nice staff here at Poly Tech came and asked us if we had time to get a bit of paperwork done at the facility. So we went along to get it out of the way, right Sophie?"

The dark-haired girl looked up when she heard her name and her eyes finally settled on Tess. "Of course! We wanted to help out as much as possible. We didn't think you'd mind, Tesla dear."

Something was very wrong here. Sophie had never called her Tesla a day in her life. She knew her friend hated her full name.

"The table was knocked over. The wine steward brought you a bottle and it broke. Come on, you guys! She saw them drag you out, kicking and screaming. Don't you remember?" She looked at Ryan again and his face was clouded in thought.

"No, he doesn't remember." Sophie pushed her chair out forcefully and stood. "He's the one who got us into this mess to begin with, losing that folder at the damn nightclub. Or have you selectively forgotten that as well, sweetie?"

Tess was stunned by the coldness in her tone. She'd never heard Sophie speak like that before. In fact, she barely recognized her friend at all, confidently wearing the skimpy blue gown she had given her earlier at the hotel. Ryan hung his head and walked back to his seat. Tess's heart was breaking for him and she couldn't think of anything he might have done to cause Sophie to treat him in such an uncivil way.

"I'd like to have a word with you, now." She went to the place where her friend stood and pulled her by the arm toward the kitchen. The girl didn't resist but she didn't look happy about it either. Once they were on the other side of the door she spun her around to face her.

"What is wrong with you?" Tess felt like shaking her, until she saw the tears streaming down her friend's face. "Tess?" Sophie looked at her like she was seeing her for the first time that evening. "Tess, oh I am sorry! I don't know what came over me. What did I just do?"

"I don't know what you were doing, but you weren't being very nice to Ryan while you were doing it."

"It was like I was watching a movie or something. Everything just came out of me, but it wasn't what I wanted to say. I kind of get the feeling I've seen Mr. Laconia before, but I can't think where." Sophie shivered and rubbed her bare arms. She looked down at the dress that barely covered her figure and blushed before looking over Tesla's attire. "Is that my sweater you have on?"

"Well, yes it is. You traded me for the dress you're wearing. Don't you remember?" Tess could tell as soon as she said the words that Sophie didn't. She had the same look on her face that Ryan did when she mentioned the wine steward.

"Please don't be mad, but do you think I could borrow it back for a bit? I don't even remember putting your outfit on, really. I'm freezing right now."

"Yes, you can. You can have anything you want. I'm sorry I yelled at you." Tess quickly unbuttoned the cardigan and wrapped it around her friend's shoulders. "Listen, I think we all need to eat, but let's make it quick. I want you and Ryan to come to my room as soon as possible. We need to regroup and figure out what's going on here."

"I couldn't agree more. I feel so bad for what I said to Ryan. Do you think he'll forgive me? Will you help me make it better with him?"

"I can tell he cares for you a lot, Sophie. We'll get through this together and you'll know how much you mean to him then." Tess walked back to the table with her arm around Sophie and was relieved when her friend sat next to her. The previous seat she'd occupied, hip to hip with Emory Laconia, still left her with an uncomfortable feeling.

Tess was deciding how they could make small talk while they ate when another person entered the room. He was older than the present group gathered at the table, and very neatly dressed. The way he carried himself said military to Tess. She thought he must be, with his closely shaved head and piercing blue eyes that didn't miss a detail as he swept them over the dinner party.

"Ah, so good of you to join us Mr. Chelsith. We were in need of new blood for the conversation." Mr. Laconia stood and shook hands with the newcomer before he was seated.

Ah, so this is his trusted head of security. If these re-

ally are bad guys they are the most polite ones I've ever seen, Tess thought.

"Oh my, it's a bit warm in here." Sophie pushed her plate away and slipped the sweater off her shoulders. "I'm not sure I'm feeling very well at the moment."

Ryan looked up from his half eaten meal with hope in his eyes. "I could take you back to you room, if you like. I'm finished here anyway."

"Oh, do you think you can actually remember where it is?" Sophie's head swiveled on her shoulders like something out of *The Exorcist* and she fixed her eyes on Ryan.

Tess couldn't believe what she was seeing. It was the same cold performance they were treated to earlier. She sharply elbowed her friend in the side. "Gosh, I'm sorry. Anyway, I thought the three of us were going to head back to my room for a drink before we turned in?"

"With him?" Sophie looked down her nose at Ryan like she was the Queen before turning to the head of Poly Tech security. "Mr. Chelsith, may I trust you to see me safely back to my suite?"

"It would be my pleasure, Sophie." The older gentleman set his napkin on the table before he'd had anything to eat. "I enjoyed your company immensely as you prepared for dinner earlier this evening. The least I can do is take you back to your room."

"What the heck?" Tess mouthed silently to Ryan across the table, who shrugged helplessly as the woman he adored walked out of the room without a glance over her shoulder. She was about to ask Mr. Laconia what was going on until she saw the look of curiosity on his face. He stood at the head of the table before she could speak.

"If you'll excuse me, Tess and Ryan, I think I'll check in with Sophie's doctor before she goes to sleep. She looks well, but I was told her head hurt quite a lot earlier. Perhaps after some sleep she'll feel herself again."

"Why don't you tell us which room she's in, so we can stop by later and make sure she's okay." Tess didn't put her request in the form of a question, because she really wasn't going to accept anything but the information.

Emory Laconia frowned almost imperceptibly, but Tess caught it as he came around the table to her.

"She could be in the medical ward later, or asleep with any luck. Why don't you let me stop by after a while and let you know what the doctor says? If she requires rest, we should let her have it, don't you think?"

No I don't, let me see her! Tess wanted to belt out the words that throbbed in her brain. If she said them, though, it would look like she didn't care about Sophie's well being—as would turning down his offer to come by her suite later. She only had one option at this point, and that was to force Ryan to sit with her until Mr. Laconia came with his news. It was probably a good idea, too, because he didn't look like he would do well to be alone now, either.

•

The last car in the security procession pulled out of the precinct parking lot and Simon was in it. His heart pounded in his chest and it took all his focus to control his breathing so he appeared normal on the outside. Two plainclothes security operatives sat in the back of the limousine with him. He wondered if either one of them might have been with the group that used the cylinder in the hall back at the resort and claimed Tess's friends.

He expected that they would notice something different about him at any moment. Any movement he made or any words he spoke could potentially give him away, so he remained still and silent. He noticed they stole a furtive glance at him more than once, but nothing sent up a red flag.

The car ride up the mountain was the most terrifying and exhilarating experience he had encountered up until this point in his memory. After everything he'd been through, that was saying a lot. He thought he couldn't be more on the edge, too, until they entered the tunnel and slowed to a stop inside the parking lot.

His car door opened and his two escorts got out first, looking around the area before they took positions on either side. He was aware of his chances when he got in the town car, and knew perfectly well this was his only way in to see Tess. Simon took the black book out of the seat pocket of the car and exited with his head held high.

"Excuse me," a strong voice called from across the open area, echoing slightly in the chamber. Simon nearly jumped out of his skin when he saw the large man striding toward him purposefully. "I'm sorry to bother you so late, sir, but you need to sign off on the new protocols before midnight and the deadline is almost upon us."

This was the end of the line. How could he sign Emory Laconia's signature? He didn't know what it looked like. He patted his pockets for a pen, trying to buy time to think, when the hulking brute in front of him chuckled gruffly.

"Very funny, Sir, you get me with that every time.

No, I don't have a pen you can borrow." He held out the pad of paper and Simon noticed it was an electronic tablet. There was no mistaking the outline of a hand displayed predominately on the screen.

Oh my god, they mean to scan my handprint! Now they'll know I'm an imposter. Simon cast a quick look around for anything he could use as a weapon, but there was nothing nearby.

Taking a deep breath, he held out his right hand palm down.

At the same time he balled his left into a fist behind his back.

Nine

"Ryan," Tess whispered to the hunched over figure on the love seat in her bedroom. She felt a little selfish, asking him to stay up all night after everything he and Sophie had just been through—whatever that was. Ryan admitted he couldn't remember all the details, but what he could recall didn't match the scene at the hotel. She knew that for sure because she'd witnessed the aftermath firsthand.

Something was wrong, but at this point Ryan wasn't going to be of any use to her in his current state of exhaustion. He probably just wanted to sleep and forget everything Sophie said that evening, and she couldn't blame him.

"Why don't you go back to your room and get some rest. It's so late, there's no way Mr. Laconia is coming back here now."

"No, wait. I'm awake. I just want to find out about Sophie before I go to sleep." Tess repressed a smile. His eyes were closed as he spoke to her and his head nodded at the end of his statement.

"I have to tell you, I'm really tired, Ryan. I'd just like to crawl into bed myself, and I can't do that with you sitting here, watching me sleep."

He lifted his head then and looked at her with red rimmed eyes. "I can sleep on the couch. If I curl up, I'll probably be able to fit. Besides, what if he does come? Then I won't be here for you, just like I wasn't for Sophie."

"I hate to tell you this, but I don't think you could protect me from the kids in the Mickey Mouse Club right now. You have to leave anyway, because I'm going to take a shower. Just get a few hours of sleep and we'll regroup then."

Tess knew once he was down he wouldn't be coming back until the morning, and that's what needed to happen. She really did intend on having a shower and resting, too. Fortunately, Ryan was a proper enough gentleman that he didn't feel right staying in while she bathed. After making her promise to call his room if she heard anything new, he headed out.

The hot water felt wonderful as it cascaded over her shoulders, soothing her tired muscles. She hadn't realized she was so sleepy until she began to slide the lavender scented soap across her skin. It was everything she could do to stay awake and she considered sitting on the wet tiles to let the stream rain down all over her.

Though she was still concerned for Sophie, she couldn't control her body as it began to shut down. All the excitement of the day was finally catching up to her and she wondered if she could even make it to the bed before she passed out.

The room was cool when she stepped out. Tess grabbed the first thing from the top dresser drawer, a pair of silk bikini underwear and matching camisole. She didn't care much about what she put on, she just longed to crawl underneath the down filled comforter and close her eyes for a few minutes.

Tess slid between the covers and sunk into the feather mattress, half asleep as she pulled the comforter up to her chin. The dim bedside lamp glowed softly and she wanted to turn it off, but her hand never made it to the button.

She was so far gone she didn't hear the lock on her door release, or see the shadow of a man standing in the hallway.

•

"I'm sorry, what did you say?" Simon was prepared to fight, not pass the security protocol. When the large man holding the notebook flipped the cover closed after the scan, Simon was stunned.

"Here is your new clearance pass for the next twenty-four hours. I apologize for being so near the deadline. I can assure you, next time I will more properly ascertain your location before we get this close. Have a good evening."

The man turned on his heel and walked briskly into an adjoining hallway on his right. Simon looked down at the key card in his hand, more frightened about what it could mean than what it might do for him at the moment. How could his hand print match that of Emory Laconia's? He knew it was impossible. Even if by some crazy chance they were identical twins, their hand and fingerprints would still differ.

Maybe they were on to him and this was a security protocol, too: lull him into a false sense of complacency and close in when he least expected it. One thing was certain. He couldn't stand here all night analyzing the situation.

Simon pocketed the badge and began to walk with feigned confidence toward the opposite side of the garage. The tiny hairs on the back of his neck stood on end when he realized he somehow knew where he was. There was no room for hesitation in his stride now. He had to go with his gut feeling. It was similar to the way he had felt when he recalled the secret caches his mixed up brain led him to the past few months.

There was a corridor up ahead, and for the first time since his accident Simon had the strangest feeling that he was coming home. Why here, of all places? All this time he never considered the possibility that maybe he belonged at the facility that held so many dangerous secrets for him.

He had tried the defenses, sure, many times. And never found a way inside. Simon didn't know if it was fear that had kept him from such a bold move like the one he performed tonight, but he suspected what had finally driven him to take the chance.

It was Tess.

Maybe he never would have taken such a risk for himself, but for her there was no question. He walked into the residential quarters, looking at all the décor with wide eyes. As his gaze swept over the pictures on the walls, his heart ached with the idea that this place was familiar. If the inkling he felt with Tess was a trickle of memory, this place brought on a waterfall of recognition.

Simon came to the bottom of the staircase, the polished rails glistening in the soft, nighttime lighting of the house. His rooms were up these stairs and at the end of the hall. He knew exactly where they were. He was almost overcome with the urge to sprint up the steps two at a time, in order to see if there was truth in his feelings. That would be a mistake. He would go slow and not attract any attention.

Simon just placed his palm on the polished curve of the banister when he heard the muted sound of footfalls behind him.

Not now, please! I'm too close to discovering the truth.

He couldn't turn around, afraid it would all be over. He recalled the distance between his position and his suite. Could he make a run for it now and get inside before he was forced to stop?

"Emory, I know it's late," the deep male voice said at his back. "I'd ask what keeps you up at this hour, but I think I know the answer to that."

"Do you, now?" He turned slowly to face the man who'd joined him at the stairs. He looked right into a piercing set of blue eyes, taking in the military hair cut and the way he stood with his hands clasped behind his back, even at ease. This was someone who knew his twin—he'd called him Emory. Would he finally be the one to realize Simon was an imposter?

"I refer to our charming guests, of course. I must say, Sophie is a lovely piece of work." The older gentleman smiled and Simon got the feeling that didn't happen very often. And what did he mean by "a lovely piece of work?" The phrase was a little unsettling.

"Yes, she certainly is," he said, intent on agreeing with everything blue-eyes had to say. He'd hoped the man would move on, but instead he peered closely at Simon's face.

"Sophie isn't the one, though, is she? You're interested in Tess, I daresay. I could tell the moment she came through on the camera feed from the hotel. The look on your face changed—you changed. In fact, you barely seem yourself right now."

Damn! That bastard Laconia wants Tess, too.

Well, he wasn't going to have her, not if he had anything to do with it. He just needed to find out where they were keeping her. Then he would make sure she and her friends were safe back at the cabin until he sorted through all of this.

"Everything is quiet now, then?" He couldn't come right out and ask where she was, he was probably supposed to know that already. His best bet was to get as much information as he could without raising any red flags.

Before the older man could answer, a radio in his pocket beeped and he drew it out. Simon clearly heard the voice at the other end address him as Mr. Chelsith, who told them to hold the line.

"Very quiet," he turned his attention back to Simon. "You know Sophie's in the medical ward, of course, and Tess is still in the suite at the top of the stairs where you left her. Ryan clicked into his own room about an hour ago, so she's probably asleep. If I were you, I'd go check on her to make sure she's tucked in safe and sound." Mr. Chelsith winked at the person he thought to be his friend. Simon's blood boiled at the gesture and he wanted to punch the lecherous old man in the face.

Maybe another time, he thought to himself, *if I'm really lucky.*

"I think I'll do just that. See to it that I'm not disturbed for the rest of the night, please." Simon moved away from the gray haired man, but not before he caught a glimpse of his knowing nod.

What kind of person was this Emory Laconia, anyway? He hoped he was nothing like him, but deep down inside, he wondered how he couldn't be. It was true; he wanted Tess more than anything in the world. But he didn't want to possess her—he wanted to be with her.

"I'm just making sure she's okay," Simon whispered to himself as he pulled the security card from his pocket. He was afraid, though. Afraid that what he was doing might be the same thing Laconia would do in his shoes … their shoes.

The door clicked and swung open without making a sound. It wasn't completely dark inside, which allowed him to see numerous rooms from his vantage point in the entryway. The dim light came from the back of the suite and after closing the door he went toward it like a moth to the flame.

Simon thought he was prepared to see her again. He'd mentally taken on the role of her rescuer and planned on being the strong, reliable type. He wasn't ready for the way his emotions sprang back to the surface, however.

Tess lay on the white dressed-out bed, deep in sleep. Her glossy red hair spilled over the pillowcase and down her shoulders where the comforter slipped away as she tossed and turned. Her lips were slightly parted, pink against the ivory skin of her face.

Simon's heart twisted painfully in his chest and he felt like a little boy again, looking at the red-haired girl in his dreams and loving her even then. Simon Says, she'd laugh, and it was all he had. Maybe that's why Tess had this kind of effect on him. She reminded him of someone who probably never existed.

He remembered how she felt with her bare back against him in the alcove of the hotel. How her heart beat against the palm of his hand when he pressed against the naked skin of her chest. Even with the danger they were in, cornered by a group of people who meant them harm, he was driven to distraction with desire for her. Simon remembered how he took the seam of her dress in his hand and fingered the material like rosary beads as he forced himself to focus on the threat against them.

He had to focus now. He didn't think it possible then, but they were all in more danger than they had ever been at the hotel. He leaned over the bed, trying to think of the gentlest way to wake the sleeping beauty without startling her.

Simon had reservations about the plan. If he did choose to rouse her, he'd have to convince her to trust him over Laconia, and he really couldn't think of any reasons why she should. He'd have to count on the connection they'd make that first night and hope that Tess would be able to sense his intentions.

"Tess," he whispered close to her left ear. When that didn't work, he brushed her bare shoulder with his fingertips. It was a last resort, because Simon was afraid that if he touched her once he'd never be able to stop.

As it turned out, he didn't have to worry about that.

"You jerk!" she said. Her eyes flew open in alarm. "What the hell are you doing in my room while I'm sleeping? I'll teach you to creep up on unsuspecting women."

Tess was out from under the blanket in a flash and Simon was too transfixed by the gracefulness of her wrath to move out of the way as she kicked him. He lost balance, arms flailing wildly before he fell flat on his back next to the bed.

"Listen, Laconia. I don't know who you think you are." She stood over him with her hands on her hips and her eyes blazing.

Just when he was sure she was going to kick his ass, she peered a little closer and cocked her head to the side. After a moment of inspection her eyes widened.

"Oh my God. It's you, isn't it, Simon?"

TEN

It was incredible.

Tess stood over Simon's sprawled figure on the floor at the end of the bed. She had wondered if she'd ever see him again, and if so, perhaps she'd realize he wasn't as similar to Emory Laconia as she'd imagined.

But that wasn't the case at all. It was true that Laconia's double appeared to be a bit worse for the wear, though if he'd been awake as long as she, that was understandable. And this version was dressed in more of a low-key military style, probably good for sneaking around hotels and heavily armed bunkers.

Damn, he's sexy in a stealthy, Navy Seal kind of way. How could one man from an identical set make her feel so different from the other? But he did. And she wasn't afraid of him, either. He'd had a multitude of chances up until this point to hurt her, and he hadn't.

He did appear to be afraid of her, though. He remained on his back, looking at her with wide eyes. At first she thought he was waiting to see if she was going to kick him again, but then she noticed the way his gaze swept over her.

Tess realized she was clothed only in a tiny silk bikini and camisole. She was so proud of herself for taking him down that fast, but the infuriating man probably liked it!

"Fine," she snapped as she crossed the room to a small closet where she took out a satin robe. "You may not be Laconia, then, but you're still a jerk! What if I'd been sleeping in the nude?"

"Are you really asking me that question?" Simon got to his feet and put his hands in his front pockets. Her eyes instinctively followed his movement and before she could stop it she found herself looking to see if perhaps she'd aroused more than his sense of humor.

Heat inflamed her cheeks and she knew she'd just put the idea in his head. He was probably imagining it now. Suddenly, even the robe wasn't enough to cover her. Oh yes, there was a big difference between the two men. Laconia never made her feel this way. In fact, he inspired the opposite sort of reaction.

"You look just like him. Or he looks like you." Tess fidgeted with the tie on her robe, still blushing too much to look him in the eye. "I mean, if both of you stand in the same spot, a hole won't open up in the space time continuum and suck us all in?"

"Please, Tess, you have to believe me. I didn't know before tonight. I'm not him, I know that much. But I also can't tell you who I am. Honestly, I was hoping you might have answers for me. I thought it couldn't be coincidence that we met and then we both ended up here."

"Me?" Tess's jaw dropped. "This is my first time here."

"Mine, too." Simon's face fell. She did believe him, then. They were both lost somehow and he'd been following her because he thought she knew something she didn't. She'd give anything to help him if she could. She understood what it was like to feel the way he did.

Tess sat on the end of the bed and Simon followed her lead, lowering himself onto the loveseat where Ryan had slept earlier.

"So, why can't you tell me who you are? Is it some kind of secret agent thing?"

He looked up at her, his lips pressed together in a hard line.

"Tess, I'm going to be completely honest with you. I can't tell you because I just don't know who I am. I dream about things—things like this facility, but I don't know why."

"We're screwed, aren't we?" It was the blind leading the blind. Tess didn't have any more control over what was happening to her or her friends than when she started.

"Not if I can help it, but we really need to get you someplace safe. There will be plenty of time for answers as long as you're all in one piece to receive them." Simon stood and there was a renewed look of purpose in his eyes. He went to the closet and pulled out her empty suitcase.

"Just get your things out of the dresser, and then we'll grab Ryan and Sophie. We'll have all three of you out in no time."

Tess watched him hurry across the room, picking up the few things she'd put on the nightstand before she went to bed. Oh, this was bad. She was going to have to tell him the truth, too.

"Hurry, the place will be up and about, soon. I heard that Chelsith guy say Sophie was in the medical ward. I can remember where that is, for some reason. And

Ryan is just nearby."

"Simon, stop, you have to listen to me. I can't leave. I think I'm the new head of Poly Tech Acquisitions."

•

He hadn't heard what she said—not clearly, anyway. She'd just told him she didn't know anything and that she'd never been to this place before. The fingers of his right hand gripped her suitcase and he couldn't let go of the luggage as he walked toward her.

"I'm sorry, Tess, you have to help me understand what you're saying." Simon came very close to her at the end of the bed, close enough to notice she was trembling. This was all falling apart and he didn't even know why. He wanted to make it okay for her, no matter what that meant for him. Even if it meant sacrificing the answers he fought so hard to obtain.

"I want to tell you, Simon." Tess stood and faced him. She was exhausted, he could see that much in the dim light, and he wanted to comfort her at the cost of everything else. "But I'm afraid if I do, it could mean something bad. Something that might make you dislike me, and I'd never even know why."

"I've never forced you to reveal anything, Tess, have I?" Simon pulled her hands away from her belt where she'd been twisting the fabric of her robe. "I have no right to and I know it. I may not have any more answers than you do, but I would give everything I have in this world if we could find them together."

Tess allowed him to keep her hands and she looked up at him with such luminous eyes he thought he could see all the way into her soul.

God, that was a sappy thing to say! Did I come on too strong? Why isn't she saying anything?

He'd never second-guessed himself as much as he had in the days that followed their first meeting in the nightclub. But then again, Simon never knew he had so much to lose, until he thought about losing her.

His mind raced over everything he'd said, the things he'd done since they first met, and he realized something that shook him to his core. He didn't care as much about finding his past as he did for his future, his future that could include this girl sitting in front of him.

Tess tightened her grip around his hands and pulled him in close. Her voice was barely a whisper and he leaned in to hear her words.

"This foundation was developed by my parents. I never knew anything about it until a few days ago. I never knew my parents, either, really. I was too young when they died. It was their wish that I inherit Poly Tech and carry on their work. I'm terrified because I don't know what that work is. I don't know anything, as a matter of fact. But I can tell you one thing ... I won't give up and I won't lose the only thing that connects me to the family I used to have."

She was so close to him, her confidential whisper hot against his cheek. He could feel the satin sleeves of her robe brush against the back of his hands as he held her fingers possessively. He believed her—every word. God help his soul if he was wrong, but he didn't care. He would tell her his only secret.

"We both must have been here as children. I think I remember you," Simon said in the same hushed tones she used. "We played together on the lawn. You laughed at me, always teasing. Do you remember me too?"

Tess froze in his arms the moment the confession left his mouth. Her eyes looked stunned and then panicked before she pulled away. He wasn't able to gauge her emotions as she let her hair fall over her face to cover her reaction. He felt more helpless than he did the first day he woke at the hospital with amnesia. Even if he wanted to take his secret back, he couldn't. Was his revelation so horrible that it could cost him the small amount of trust he thought he'd built with her?

"Tess, just look at me." He lifted her chin with his fingers, taking the chance he wouldn't spook her with such a bold move.

Please let the bond I felt with her at the start mean something, Simon thought. She leveled her chin and there was resolution in her eyes. He could feel her strength and determination and it was damn sexy.

"It's you," Tess said. "It's always been you and I know that more than I know anything else in my mysterious life. I don't know how much time I have to explain, but there are some really strange things going on you should be aware of since we're on the same side now."

She trusts me. There is nothing that can stop me now! He felt like she'd just given him the most incredible gift in the world.

"I don't know what else you can tell me that could matter more." Simon's head was dizzy with elation and he was thrown off balance by the physical reaction.

"You might be surprised." She smiled up at him with a sensual curve of her lips and he lost control of his will. The memory of her kiss on the dance floor had haunted him for days and here she was, practically in his arms. It wasn't like him, to be so helpless at the sight of a beautiful woman's mouth. He didn't think it was, anyway. Surely he was stronger than this in his previous life.

"Seriously, we have to make a plan," Tess pleaded,

but her bewitching smile stayed with her like it was a part of her spirit and he leaned in to capture her kiss before he could stop himself.

She yielded to him the moment they touched. He felt like she'd been waiting all this time, too. Though he initiated the intimacy, she pulled him in with an intensity that surprised and inflamed him in the same instant. Tess became the soul of his passion, and the feel of her skin against his drove him wild with the need for more. This wasn't the place, he knew that in the back of his mind, but his entire body vibrated with a desire that had to be slaked.

His hands roamed over the soft fabric that clung to her curves and as he brushed her thigh she moaned against his lips. Her whole body convulsed beneath him and he felt her fingernails graze the skin on the back of his neck as she arched against the length of his body.

"We have to get away from here. Let me take you someplace they can't find you." He'd never felt such a protective desire before, not even to safeguard his own neck in the recent past. Simon realized his desire to be with her was merging with a primal urge to keep this woman safe.

"I could say the same thing to you," Tess teased him between kisses. "We're probably both in the same amount of trouble. Maybe we should concentrate on saving each other."

"You are driving me crazy, woman," Simon growled deeply as he chased her lips to prove his dominance.

"You mean we're not there yet?" she said in a husky tone, and somehow that was sexier than anything she'd done to him so far. He didn't think either of them was getting away tonight and he sure couldn't vouch for

Tess's safety in his arms.

A sharp click from the door to the room knocked him back to his senses. He straightened with his hands still on Tess. She'd heard it too and she covered her mouth to stifle a gasp. The handle moved almost imperceptibly in the gloom, but it didn't open.

The click again, followed by silence.

Simon put his hand in his right jacket pocket and felt the access card he'd been given in the parking garage. New security protocols at midnight. And there was only one person at the facility that didn't get his badge updated. Simon knew all too well whose card he received.

Emory Laconia was on the other side of the door and chances were pretty good he wasn't happy right now.

ELEVEN

Oh, thank God the door didn't open! She had no idea who was on the other side, but she was starting to get pissed about the open door policy her suite apparently came with.

"What the hell is this?" Tess tried to keep it down but her voice hissed out sharply. "How many people have access to my room? I am never going to be able to sleep in this place."

Simon's eyes widened when she yanked her arms out of his hold and crossed them in front of her chest. He shook his head and then he held up his hands in surrender.

"Hey, just don't kick me again. This isn't really mine." He took a card out of his pocket and gave it to her quickly. "Someone handed this to me when I first got here and said it was the new security protocols. There isn't a name anywhere, but I can guess who is almost as ruggedly handsome as me and might have access to every room in the building."

She turned the plastic key card over in her hands. It wasn't magnetic; it was the type of code a laser would scan. It looked like the one she was given to unlock her door, but it had different colored strips below the encrypted data patterns on the back.

"I believe you, Simon. If we're going to work together, we have to trust each other." Tess held the card out to him between two fingers. "Now take this and get out of here quick before someone decides to come back with the right code."

"What do you mean, get out? You're forgetting about the part where I came here to rescue you—you know that, right? " He cocked his head to the side and his eyebrows furrowed.

Damn, he's sexy when he's trying to be chivalrous, Tess sighed inwardly. *Maybe not too bright, though.* She was going to have to spell things out for him.

"You said it yourself. We have a pass here with twenty-four-hour access to everything in the facility. I recall a conversation where you informed me you were seeking answers ... in this facility. Do you follow me?"

Simon frowned and looked away from her. He paced over to the door and listened for a minute before he returned through the hall to the bedroom.

"I don't think I could live with myself if something happened to you while I was out there selfishly looking into my own past." He crossed his arms and adopted the same stubborn stance she had.

"I'm supposed to be here, remember? If I go missing, or any of my friends for that matter, you're not going to get very far with that pass. You have twenty-four hours. A little less, now because of the, um, lengthy introductions in my room tonight."

Tess forced herself to focus, but she was still breathless from the intimate encounter moments before. He had to listen to her. They both had a lot at stake here, but how could she leave when she'd just arrived? This was all she had of her own past and she couldn't run now. He could help them both by taking advantage of this opportunity they'd been given.

"Dammit, I'll do as you say." His eyes were dangerously dark. "Not because I want to, or it's the right choice, but because I don't think I can deny you anything you want from me."

Her spine tingled when he said those words. She was torn between her desire for him and knowledge of her family. He was so close to her right now, almost touching. His eyes searched her face and she bit her lip to keep it from trembling in front of him.

Because Tess had grown up alone, she'd raised herself. She learned to be strong at an early age and had never regretted it. And she was the strongest she'd ever been when she resisted the urge to reach out to him and pull him back into her arms. To whisper to him that they would go away together now and she would trust in him to keep her safe.

But where would that leave Simon? She knew her feelings for him were not fleeting. He might come to regret it later if he didn't take this chance for himself.

"Just remember, you're doing this for both of us." She pulled back a little when he leaned forward for a kiss and a look of disappointment passed across his face. It wasn't that she didn't want him to kiss her. She was afraid she wouldn't want him to stop.

"I know. I have less than twenty-four hours, now." He followed the hall and listened at the door again before he put his fingers on the handle.

"Tess." She saw him smile over his shoulder in the dark as he cracked the door. "The hour was worth it. It's been great meeting you."

She walked toward him to see him out safely, but her legs froze as he slipped through the opening into the hall and collided with a dark figure just outside the door.

•

Careless fool!

Simon was so busy looking behind at the woman he loved that he didn't make sure the hallway was clear before he blundered out into the corridor. He was stunned by the mistake and didn't react for a moment. That might have been what saved him. Simon stared down into the face of the dark-haired girl he'd seen with Tess at the nightclub, on what he liked to think of as their first date.

This must be Sophie. Will she remember me from the dance floor? Will she give me away?

"Emory!" The petite girl reacted with astonishment. "I mean … Mr. Laconia. I thought you had gone to bed for the evening?"

Oh, she remembered him all right—the other him. This was starting to get a little annoying, but he had to remember to use his advantage whenever he could.

"I was just checking on Tesla to make sure she was settled in and had everything she needed. And as it all seems in order, I'll just be going."

"I see." Sophie pouted. She pushed by him with a cold shoulder and he got the feeling she was upset about him being there. "I came to see Tess as well. I couldn't sleep and I thought she and I could lie in bed and talk for a while, like we used to in school. That always helped me."

Simon turned his back to the brightly lit hall. He

watched as Sophie slipped into the gloom of Tess's suite and put her arm around her friend's shoulder. It was dark, but Simon thought he saw Tess shiver.

"So, if you don't need anything else?" He threw the question out tentatively. He almost hoped Tess would ask him not to leave her alone with this person who was supposed to be her friend. He couldn't put his finger on it, but she didn't seem as warm and friendly as she had that night by the dance floor.

"No, I'm good." Tess nodded and put her hand on the door knob. "I'll take care of things here. You have more than enough to do."

She stressed the word *enough* when she said it, reminding him of the dangerous task ahead. Simon knew what he had to do was incredibly risky, but somehow he was more concerned with Tess and her new Stepford-Wife bed buddy. Maybe his judgment was clouded by his feelings for her and he was seeing threats to her safety everywhere.

He figured there was only one way to find out. Chelsith said Sophie had been in the medical ward. Maybe she had a condition he didn't know about. He could at least go by there and look at her file. There could even be something about his past there as well. If he was here before and had been ill, there would surely be records. At least it was a place to start.

Once the door was closed he looked both ways down the hall before he proceeded to the staircase. Simon had to constantly remind himself to act natural. There were probably security cameras everywhere. He had a much better chance navigating the facility if he acted calm and confident.

He knew where to go. It didn't feel like it was from

memory. More like a dream where he'd been someone else and that was unsettling. All this time he'd been searching for answers, he'd never had anyone to worry about except himself. Things were going so well with Tess. What if he discovered something terrible about his past that could change that?

He came to an elevator he had seen in his mind a thousand times before. The exterior had no buttons or controls to access, just a blank computer screen. Without thinking about it, Simon pulled out his key card and scanned the code underneath the small pad.

The grey screen lit up and offered a list of floors with a flashing prompt next to his current location. The medical ward was sub-level three. Not at the bottom, but very close.

Must be where they want to keep things they don't want getting out, he thought, feeling confined as he stepped into the cage. This was absolute security, nothing on the inside of the carriage but smooth walls. *No way out if they wanted to stop you. Cameras in here too,* he thought for sure. *Act normal.*

He checked his watch and feigned boredom as the elevator descended in silence. It was still early. Maybe the staff would be minimal in the ward and he could access the records in private. All the while he knew at any moment they could discover the protocol mix-up and his heart pumped dizzying amounts of blood through his veins.

The doors opened and he got a visual of the dimly lit corridor before he stepped out.

Learned that lesson, at least.

The silence was thick in the air as he walked along the plush carpet to the double doors at the end of the hall. Another scanner was mounted to the right side and he flashed his card before he could change his mind.

It was all or nothing. And right now, he was angling for all of it.

He entered the ward like he owned the place. Hell, for all he knew, he did. At least until Tess took over. He didn't like her odds against Laconia, but he was going to do what he could to even them.

"Excuse me." The soft voice at his elbow startled him despite his well maintained composure.

And who wouldn't be startled? The young girl behind the desk was so small he hadn't seen the top of her head over the counter. Were they making Leprechauns down here or what? He had to rein in his nervous thoughts before they spun out of control.

"I'm sorry," he started out, apologizing for what she hadn't even heard. Before he could get any further she jumped up and came around the desk. She was a fair-haired girl with freckles, and the look of distress on her face was unmistakable.

"Oh, Mr. Laconia! Wow, I can't believe you're here. I know I'm supposed to be standing when you come in, but we weren't expecting you. Is there anything I can get you?"

"It's quite alright. I wasn't expected." She was anxious and he wanted to set her at ease. She might be able to help him. "I'm sorry, what was your name?"

"Um, it's Trudy. But you wouldn't know that. We've never met. You hate coming down here ...Well, I was told."

"I am very glad to meet you, Trudy." Simon flashed his most charismatic smile. The girl was beside herself and kept covering her mouth with her tiny hands. He didn't know if she was smiling or gaping at him behind her fingers.

When she didn't speak for another minute he nodded at her, to move things along. "Right. I wanted to check on Sophie's file, if you're not too busy?"

"I can pull that file for you right now, Mr. Laconia." Trudy nodded back at him with a dazzled smile. "Do you want to see her as well?"

Did I hear that right? What is she talking about? He knew a look of confusion crossed his face for a second. *God, don't let me come this far and give it away. Get control of yourself now!*

"It's okay, Mr. Laconia. You don't have to see her. I just thought you might want to." Trudy was nervous now and he didn't blame her. He had to smooth it over fast.

"You know, I wasn't going to. Now that you mention it, though, I think I will. What a great idea, Trudy." He lavished heavy praise on her with his voice and she responded immediately.

"Thanks! I'll take you in to her room and then get that file. I think you'll be happy with her status." She turned and began walking through one of the corridors behind the desk. He followed her like it was the most normal thing in the world. "She's been at Grade One for the past ten hours."

Ten hours? That couldn't be right. He kept a stone face as Trudy scanned her own card at the door and they entered a large room filled with shadows. He walked to the bed in the far corner of the room, the obvious focal point of the area.

"As you can see, she's settled completely. We don't expect any more occurrences. I'll be right back with her stats."

Trudy left the room, but Simon didn't hear a word she said. He couldn't think—he couldn't move as he looked at the figure in the hospital bed.

It was Sophie. Pale and sick looking, hooked up to wires and tubes in all of her extremities, but there was no doubt about her identity. His fingers grasped the cold metal rail along the bed until his knuckles turned white. He only had one thought in his head.

If this was Sophie, who the hell was in Tess's room right now?

TWELVE

This isn't Sophie.

Tess had chills all over her body at the thought she couldn't push out of her mind. The strange things was, Sophie seemed to be herself at times. But when she wasn't … holy crap—get the chainsaw.

Her dark hair was disheveled and she hugged the cardigan she'd borrowed back from Tess across her chest. It didn't really matter what Tess thought right now. After everything the two of them had been through together, she wasn't going to turn on her best friend now no matter how oddly she was behaving. She would just have to figure out what was wrong.

"Listen, come over to the sofa and sit down for a minute. We can talk, like we used to late at night." Tess put her hands on Sophie's shoulders and it was like touching a stranger. The girl flinched, almost imperceptibly, but allowed Tess to move her toward the couch.

"Sophie, you've been acting differently ever since we got separated at the hotel. Did something happen that you're not telling me?" Tess perched on the edge of the couch and watched as her friend covered her face with her hands.

"I'm just tired, okay?" She said the words through her fingers and began to lightly rock back and forth against the cushions.

"I know, I'm tired, too," Tess said. She reached out to take Sophie's hand. Maybe they both needed a good night's sleep.

"Why is everything always about you?" Sophie shrilly exploded into action, slapping Tess's hand away and jumping to her feet. "You don't know what I've been through since we got here!"

"No, no I don't know." Tess stood to face her friend, her stomach churning from the unprovoked outburst. "If you'd just tell me, we can fix it."

"It's this headache," she mumbled, before turning her back on Tess and stumbling to the bed. "I've had it ever since I got here. I've tried to sleep, believe me. Every time I close my eyes I have terrible dreams. There are needles and an operating room. It feels like I've been in an accident."

"Oh God, why didn't you tell me this at dinner?" Tess was afraid now, really afraid, for the first time since they got here. Before this admission, Poly Tech had been an intriguing mystery. Now the reality of Sophie's condition hit home for her. If she was sick, would they even let her leave?

All she had was Simon—thank goodness she hadn't given him away. She knew he had the means to remove them from the facility. And that was exactly what she was going to ask him to do. There were other ways to find out about her parents, and even if there weren't, she wasn't going to risk her friend to stay here.

Crazy experimental facility, minus one. Tess, zero. This game was over.

"Hey, we're going to go home, okay? Right now." Tess went to the suitcase Simon had partially filled and slipped on some dark colored travelling clothes. She threw her other things to the side. She wasn't planning on taking anything with her, other than her friends.

"Can I just rest for a minute, please? I'm so tired." Sophie crawled on top of the comforter on the bed and looked at Tess with heavily lidded eyes.

Tess glanced at the door and wondered how long it would be before Simon returned. They couldn't leave without him and Ryan, anyway. "I guess it's alright if we lie down for a few."

Her brain kept telling her it was still dark outside, time to sleep. But they were underground and judging by her watch it was probably dawn. Still, she was past the point of exhaustion. As long as she had Sophie where she could protect her, what harm could come from relaxing a little until Simon came back for them?

Tess went to the other side of the bed and reclined on top of the covers. Her body was filled with tension. Even with the stress she felt, she started to nod off right away. She looked at Sophie on the other side and the girl was out like a light, though she tossed and turned fitfully.

It was okay. She wouldn't sleep—she'd just close her eyes for a minute and relax.

"Tess, will you snuggle with me?" The voice drifted to her ears from far away and she sat straight up. Her heart pounded painfully and she wondered how long she'd been out. When she got her bearings she realized Sophie had come very close to her on the bed. Even in the dark she could see the pain in her eyes. That headache must be killing her.

"That's a strange thing to ask, don't you think?" Tess was confused by her request. This wasn't like her friend at all, but nothing about their circumstances was familiar now.

"I know. I'm sorry. It's just that my head hurts so much. I don't know how to make it feel better."

Her voice was sincere, and she sounded like Sophie. But why didn't she feel like her? Tess couldn't put her finger on it, but the sooner they all got out of there the better.

"Okay, come here." Tess opened her arms. She had no reason to be afraid of this person she'd known for most of her adult life. Sophie had never hurt her or given her cause for concern.

Still ... she thought as Sophie curled up next to her. *Please don't let there be an ice pick under the bed.*

Tess stroked the soft hair that fell across Sophie's temple. It wasn't long before the rhythmic motion lulled her into a relaxed state and she started to drift off.

She was just beginning to forget everything again. To let go and allow the warm darkness fall over her, when she felt the touch of skin against her lips. Tess's eyes flew open and she saw Sophie leaning over her, tenderly kissing her mouth.

"What the hell are you doing?" She abruptly pushed the girl away, too shocked and confused to even get up. The skin on her face felt numb and her brain could barely process what just happened.

"I'm sorry, Tess! I don't know ... I don't know what I'm doing." Sophie jumped off the mattress. "Please don't be mad at me. I think maybe I'm crazy. My thoughts are all fragmented and sometimes I think terrible things. I don't feel like myself anymore. I don't feel like anyone."

The sobbing girl collapsed in a heap on the floor alongside the bed.

This was way past the boundary of their friendship. It wasn't even in the realm of reality. She knew she could go over to the distraught girl and make her feel better, but what would happen the next time she fell asleep? There was only one thing she could think to do.

"Sophie, I think you just need to rest." Tess walked over to the table where she kept her purse. "I know you've never liked taking medication, but I still have a few of those sleeping pills the doctor gave me when I was stressed over my thesis. Would you consider taking one?"

Sophie's pale, puffy face peeked over the side of the mattress.

"How many do you have?"

•

"Here's your file, Mr. Laconia." Trudy had entered the room so silently Simon hadn't been aware of her presence. He wondered how long she'd been standing there before she addressed him.

His movements were slow as he turned to accept the case she held out. It was heavy, some type of fireproof metal, he knew. He'd seen it before, somewhere. Probably here. There was a biometric scanner along the edge and he knew his thumbprint would unlock the contents.

"I really hope she'll be all right." Trudy slid past him and gently brushed a wisp of hair from Sophie's face. Her voice was filled with genuine concern and Simon watched the emotion on her face when she patted the comatose girl's hand.

"She was so frightened when they brought her in, but even though she was dying, she was kind to everyone here." She smiled at him and sighed. "They told me they'd let me know how her imprint was doing. I mean, it was such a rush job and everything. You know how Research & Development is, though. They never got back to me. Anyway, I'm just glad her husband made it. He's probably still under observation, but I'm still surprised he hasn't been down to see his wife since the accident."

Whoa! Her husband? Did the girl mean Ryan? Simon had a feeling Trudy didn't know much more of the real story than he did. He had to get back to Tess right away and let her know what was going on.

"Trudy, I have an early morning meeting, but I promise I'll be back when it's finished and we can talk about this in more depth." He turned before she could get another word out, but as he reached the door she called out to him.

"Mr. Laconia, thank you, but you can't take the file out of the medical ward. It's a very strict policy."

He swung around to face the petite girl and wondered if he'd have to use force to silence her. It was the last thing he wanted to do and he'd make sure he didn't hurt her, but he had to get out of there now. He searched her eyes for a clue as to what her next move might be. She blushed and lowered her gaze in response.

"Well, I guess you know the rules. You made them, right?" She laughed nervously and shrugged in apology. "Besides, you're coming back shortly, right? You can bring the file then."

•

Simon hurried through the corridor toward the elevator. It was already later than he'd like and there were sure to be more people up and about. The moment that bastard Laconia realized his old pass was no good he'd be screwed. It was tempting to open the file and take a moment to glance over the information. He could be caught at any moment and if they took it away before he cracked it open this whole mission was for nothing. Even then, all he could think about was Tess and what kind of danger she was in, alone with that Sophie look-alike.

Is that what she is, a look-alike? Is that what I am, too?

Fear knotted his stomach from the possible ramifications of the thought, and he pushed it to the back of his mind. He didn't matter right now. Only Tess. He tried to keep the signs of relief from crossing his face as the elevator accepted his key card. He had to remain calm and maintain his composure just a little while longer.

He couldn't feel the car ascend. The machinery didn't make a sound and he felt a moment of panic. Had they discovered him already and stopped the elevator? Would there be someone waiting for him on the other side and he'd never make it to her?

Simon braced himself for a confrontation, but when the doors slid open the hall was empty. He was on the residential floor, and so far he didn't see anyone. Tess's room was right around the corner and though he wanted to run, he walked with even, measured strides.

He'd let himself in before, but now he felt it would be rude after her reaction the first time. With his pass in hand, he knocked lightly. No answer. Simon drew a breath and hammered out a firm rap. It was louder than he intended, driven by his anxiety. Still, no answer. Was she in danger? Maybe he was too late after all.

He scanned the card and forced himself to turn the handle slowly. He slipped inside and closed the door, resting his back against the wood so he could steady himself to listen. There was nothing.

Simon moved deeper into her suite, using the same glow from the tiny lamp in her bedroom as a guide. There was a figure on the bed, covered with blankets, lying as still as the grave. His heart leapt into his throat and he sprang forward.

"Tess." His voice choked up when he said her name. He placed his hands on her shoulders. "Please be okay."

"I'm fine, but Sophie isn't."

Simon spun around to see Tess on the sofa, propped up against a handful of pillows and covered with a jacket. He didn't realize he'd been holding his breath until it rushed out in relief.

"Listen, that's not Sophie. You have to understand me. I don't know who—or what—she is, but this person isn't your best friend."

Tess sat up and shook her head. Her eyes were still glazed from sleep and she looked at him like he was a little bit crazy. Maybe he was.

"You know, I normally wouldn't believe something like that. But I've just spent a little time with her and I can at least agree she'd not herself. That's for sure."

"I just came from the medical ward. Sophie was there, but she wasn't conscious. They said she'd been in some kind of accident." Simon sat close to her on the couch and looked into her eyes.

"An accident?" Tess looked at the figure on the bed and her brow furrowed.

"She had an IV and there was a lot of equipment monitoring her stats. I'm not sure what is really going on, but the nurse attending her really believed that."

"So ... you're telling me there are two Sophies and one of them is a fake? You think it's her?" Tess nodded at the sleeping girl across the room.

"You tell me. You said yourself she'd been behaving strangely. I know how all of this must sound, so trust your instincts. What do you feel?"

Tess stood and walked to the side of the bed. He could sense her reasoning, thinking through the information at hand. She was damn smart, an impressive woman. When he first saw her he thought she was stunningly beautiful, but her strength and character through all of this made her magnificent in his eyes.

The decision didn't take long. "Okay, I believe you. Now take me to see Sophie."

She walked across the room and picked up her purse before he could blink, but he was hesitant. It was one thing to go tromping about the compound himself, but having her at his side made it a lot more risky.

"I just looked at the clock on the nightstand. It's almost eight AM. There will be a lot of people between here and there pretty soon. Are you sure you want to take that chance?"

She looked at him like he was slow. "Are you really asking me that? Let's go, we're wasting time talking about it. Besides, it wouldn't be the first time others saw Emory walking me through the corridor."

"Emory? You're on a first name basis with him now?" Simon frowned as they entered the hall.

"Well, not exactly. But fake Sophie apparently is. It makes me a little nauseated, if you really want to know." They turned right and Simon felt a small sense of satisfaction. At least she seemed as distrustful of the guy as he was. When they reached the elevator Simon scanned his pass and the interface lit up. She could see he chose sublevel three. Neither of them said a word during the ride below.

"It's down this hall," he whispered under his breath and Tess nodded. The passage seemed so much longer than it did the first time he was down here. It couldn't have been more than half an hour ago, but it felt like days.

He had the pass ready in his hand and ran the card under the infrared beam. This time, the green light didn't come on and he didn't hear the tumbler unlock.

"Crap." Simon passed it through again, and this time the pad emitted a jarring beep. The symbol of a lock flashed across the screen and he knew he was caught.

"Here, try my key. I don't know if it will work, but it's worth a shot." She fumbled in her purse and pulled out the card, but he stuffed it back inside.

"Tess, they can't know you were with me. If we try your card there will be a record of it. Right now you just wandered into the wrong part of the facility." He glanced down the hall, wondering how long it would be until security arrived.

"There are cameras, I'll bet. They'll see I was with you anyway."

"True, but security might pass me off as Laconia. I have to disappear, right now." He walked to the closest door and reached for the handle. A loud click rang off the metal and he knew it locked beneath his grip. The cascading sound of turning locks came one after another, like a domino effect down the long corridor.

"Come on, run!" He grabbed Tess's hand as they tried to outdistance the lockdown protocol. They were almost out of options when Simon grabbed the nearest knob and found it open. They blundered into the small space without looking ahead.

It was dark inside, and close. From the smell of chemicals they were in some kind of cleaning closet. Better than nothing. At least there was a knob on the door he could use.

"Tess, listen to me," he whispered as he took the copper cylinder out of his pocket and turned it on. "They can't realize you know about Sophie. And they can't know we were together."

"Wait, what do you mean, were?" She grabbed his wrist and held it with a firm grasp. "Where are you going?"

"If they find you with this case, you're going to be in terrible danger. More than I'd imagined before I got here." Simon attached the end of the cylinder to the knob and stepped back as it sparked and whirled furiously. "I know you won't leave without your friends. I'll be back and I'll have a way to get you all out."

He opened the door and the familiar smell of the musty cabin greeted him. He had less than a minute after he sliced the doorway, but he found it difficult to go through.

"Wait," she said in a panic. "Can you get back here, anytime you want?"

"Now that I've accessed this doorway from the inside, the device will map the location. I promise I'll be back for you."

Tess backed against the far wall of the closet. He thought she was getting out of his way. Before he could exit she sprang forward into his arms. The unexpected momentum caught him off guard and he fell backward.

Simon automatically released the case and the device on the door. His arms encircled her waist, the instinct to protect her stronger than anything else.

He felt her breath on his cheek as he fell back and took the full force of their weight. "We stay together from now on."

It was the last thing he heard before he hit his head on the hardwood floor of the cabin.

THIRTEEN

Tess felt them falling into the black on the other side of the door. She was afraid and exhilarated at the same time. Simon wouldn't have opened the area if he hadn't been sure it was safe. Still, it felt like a long way down.

She heard the hard case he'd been carrying smack the floor behind him and slide, just a second before they landed on the solid surface. His breath whooshed out of his chest beneath her, brushing over her face. She tried to roll off him, but not before she heard the thud of his head hitting wood. There was a sickening snap and she prayed it was his jaw rocketing shut and not a skull fracture.

He took the brunt of their combined weight. She lay on her side next to him, her hip bone bruised from the small impact she took by flipping off of him. *If it hurt me this much, how must he feel?*

"Simon, are you all right?" Her voice fell flat in the void. She couldn't hear him breathing. Tess fumbled across his chest with her fingers and didn't detect any rise or fall. If something happened to him, it was her fault. She didn't mean to knock him off balance. She just hadn't wanted him to leave without her again.

"Oh God, Tess?" He moaned under his breath. "If you wanted to come, all you had to do was ask."

She felt terrible. It was just an accident, but she was still responsible.

"I'm so sorry, Simon. Hurting you was the last thing I had on my mind when I flung myself into your arms." She shivered and realized it wasn't just dark; it was freezing cold as well.

"I kind of liked that part, actually. The flinging ... not the landing." She felt his muscles flex underneath her fingertips and knew he was trying to sit up. He didn't make it far.

"I can't see a thing in here. Can you tell me where the light switch is?" She crawled up onto her hands and knees to feel around.

"I'm still seeing stars, actually. But I'd rather be seeing you. This cabin is pretty small, so when you hit a wall you won't have far to go. There's a small closet, about two feet wide. You'll find a flashlight on the top shelf."

"Are you flirting with me or is it just the head injury talking?" Tess wanted to keep up the playful banter until she could get a good look at Simon's cranium. Besides, she really wanted to know the answer to that question.

"That depends. Do you like it or not?" He groaned and she heard him shift his weight again as she ran her hand along the wall.

"Well, let's see what I know about you." She came across the closet and opened the door. It was a little unnerving, reaching her hand into a cold, black hole, but the flashlight was where he said it would be.

"You're a good dancer, I noticed that right off. Nice dresser, too. Not bad looking... Yes, you may continue to flirt with me." Tess pointed the light at the floor before she turned it on. She didn't want to blind him, too.

"There's an end table next to the sofa. Turn that lamp on and if it's not burned out, you'll be able to see more." She swept the beam over his figure and noticed he'd managed to prop himself up. That was a good sign. From her vantage point, the cabin was tiny. The sofa was the largest thing in the room. Even though the lamp was small, it put out a lot of light in the close area. She was pretty happy to see a fireplace in the corner, even though it didn't look it had been used for a while.

"If there's no heater in this place, and I'm betting there isn't, can we get a fire going over there?"

"Honestly, I don't know if there's any wood. I've never lit the thing, myself."

Tess switched off the flashlight and set it on the end table. "So, this isn't your babe lair, then?"

"From all the places I've been, I'm pretty sure I don't have one." Simon smiled at her when she came over to help him to the couch. Her heart fluttered in her chest and she wondered if the feeling would ever wear off.

"If this hurts, let me know." She sat next to him and reached up to feel the back of his head. He leaned forward a little and though he didn't say anything, she felt him wince when she ran her fingers across the swelling.

"I supposed you'd need to have your arms cut off before you'd admit something hurts, right?" She said.

Strong, silent type, then ... Yummy.

Snap out of it, girl! You guys are in trouble and you're sitting here with romantic fantasies cropping up like there's nothing wrong.

"You're next to me on a love seat, running your fingers through my hair, and you think I can feel any pain?"

The corner of his mouth turned up and Tess found it hard to focus.

She shivered from the cold and instinctively leaned in close to Simon. Her heart raced as he searched her eyes for motive. She knew she wanted more from him than his survival skills, but even she had to admit the timing couldn't be worse. The truth was, she was exhausted. Her decision making capabilities were probably at their lowest. It had to be the reason she felt light-headed from his masculine scent that clung to her hands and clothing.

"I'm a terrible host." He stood slowly and she felt cold where she'd been touching him before. "I'll go outside and see if there is any firewood. At the very least, we're in the middle of a forest. Something should be lying around."

"Well, that's one thing you can do, I guess ..." Oh my God, did I just pout? I hope he didn't see that!

"You still want the fire, right?" He turned to her with his hand on the door knob.

If she said no it would sound ridiculous, so she nodded her head. She could do with a few minutes alone to get herself together, anyway. She'd just stretch out on the couch and close her eyes until he came back.

It felt like seconds had passed, but Simon came back in the door with an armload of wood. He walked past her and knelt on the hearth with his back to the room. His muscular thighs flexed as he rocked back on his heels and Tess felt a wave of desire wash over her. She wanted to come up behind him, run her hands over his strong shoulders and touch his biceps through the soft cable knit sweater. A small tickling sensation formed in her stomach. It spread down her thighs and settled into her abdomen with an ache so deep it took her by surprise.

The flame caught right away and she felt the warmth as it filtered past Simon. He lingered to tend it a few minutes longer before he turned to look at her over his shoulder.

"You're watching me." He smiled shyly and Tess's heart almost burst with tenderness at the look on his face. She got the idea he didn't entertain company very often.

"There's no TV," she teased, holding his gaze as he crept over to the couch and sat next to her on the floor.

"I've got more bad news—there's no hot tub, either." He briefly rubbed his eyes with his fingertips. He was probably as tired as she was and he was injured, thanks to her.

"Let me see if that goose egg of yours is any bigger." Tess turned his head to face the fire and fanned her fingers out at the base of his skull, working upward. His hair was thick and silky. She found herself stroking his scalp lightly as she moved to the swelling.

"Mmm, that feels so good, Tess." His voice was heavy and sensual. The sound of it sent shivers through her veins and she wanted to give him more.

Tess touched the side of his jaw with the fingertips of her free hand and when he didn't pull away, she slipped inside the collar of his turtleneck. He inhaled sharply when she touched his hot skin but she couldn't stop herself.

His body was exquisitely wrought, hard and defined under her hands. Her fingers clenched against his scalp, lightly pulling his thick hair in a rhythmic motion that matched her shallow breathing.

"Oh God, Tess, do you know what you're doing to me?" He could barely breathe the words out and she felt his heart hammer against her palm.

"That depends," she leaned forward and whispered, her soft lips brushing against his ear. "Do you like it?"

His whole body trembled in reaction and he gasped. Before she could go any further, he gently removed her hands and held them as he sat on the couch next to her.

"Look at me, Tess." He was serious, struggling to regain his breath. "I need to tell you, I am just a man. A man who has never wanted anything more than what you're giving me now. If you continue, I won't be able to stop. There is only one thing I'm sure of in my life—I will never be able to stop loving you once I start."

"I don't want you to stop." She held his gaze so he would know she meant every word. "Not ever."

She wanted him and needed him in every way she could imagine. In the middle of her crazy life, being with him was suddenly the only thing that made sense. Her heart had known it the first time she saw his face in London, and her soul accepted it now.

Tess kneeled next to him on the couch and pulled the waistband of his sweater over his head and off his arms. He looked at her with wide eyes as she tossed it to the side. She wrapped her hands around his neck and leaned down to touch his lips. He let her explore at first, but the more contact she made the more he pulled from her kiss.

Simon ran his strong hands up her back and captured her face, holding her captive as he delved deeper with unrestrained passion. Tess straddled his lap, pressing against his bare chest. The heat from his skin seared her through her thin T-shirt and she gyrated against him in a seamless rhythm of desire.

He kept her close as his mouth moved to her chin before he captured the pulse point on her neck. His mouth pressed against it with firm lips, grazing her skin with his teeth. Her nipples were so hard they ached and she rubbed against him through the filmy material that separated them.

"Take off my shirt." Tess raised her arms over her head. She needed him to touch her, everywhere. Simon effortlessly peeled her top away, the bra along with it. Her exposed skin broke out in gooseflesh, further hardening her nipples.

She took the back of his head in her hands and guided his mouth to her breasts. His lips were wet and he brushed them across her tight nubs and Tess thought she was going to have an orgasm right there.

"Oh god, Simon!" She threw her head back and moaned when he took her right nipple fully into his mouth and painted it with his rough tongue. He covered her left breast with his free hand, twisting her exposed nipple between his fingers and his thumb.

Tess was wet all the way through her clothes. She had never felt anything like this before in her life. She needed him inside her and she needed it now. She reached for his belt and he undid the button on her pants at the same time. They worked the remainder of their clothing down to the floor without separating, though she had no idea how they managed it.

She leaned forward, gasping as his hot, pulsing member tapped against her belly. This was no small matter but before she could gauge it, Simon took her breasts in his mouth again, holding them together and licking both her nipples at the same time.

She slid herself up and down his hard shaft, needing more and more of it as his attentions became demanding. He was slick from her desire and when she crested the top of his erection slid against her opening. She pressed down, gently at first. His size was almost more than she could take.

Simon lowered his hands to her hips and slowly began to work her more deeply onto his erection. She was so tight her pleasure point rubbed against him as she took him in. Her entire body trembled with the exquisite sensation that flooded through her veins and she knew she wasn't going to last much longer.

Tess wanted Simon to feel what she was feeling, to give him the ultimate climax he was leading her to. With a small cry of pure ecstasy, she took him all the way inside and rocked against him with wild abandon. She felt the spasms begin, her mind filling with an explosion of sensations. She was coming and she couldn't stop it now. Tess clenched around him like a vice, riding out the glorious waves of her orgasm as Simon exploded inside her. He cried out and his hands roughly ground her down onto his pulsing member.

She whimpered with satisfaction, collapsing into his arms. It was the last bit of energy she had, but she felt like it could've lit the world for the brief time they were one. Now that they were together, everything would be all right.

Simon reclined onto the couch, pulling her next to his side as he snagged a blanket from the back. She wanted to tell him how she felt, but she was fading fast. So tired.

It didn't matter anyway. Nothing could tear them apart now.

Fourteen

Simon couldn't move.

Something weighed his arms and legs down. His eyelids were heavy and he struggled to open his eyes.

Where the hell am I?

The sound of hospital equipment filled the room and he felt a moment of panic at the loss of control. He drew a ragged breath and heard a beep just above his head, matching his heart beat. His thoughts were jumbled. Had they caught him again?

"He's waking up, sir."

Clipboards snapped. Simon exerted an extreme force of will and opened his eyes a sliver. Cold, fluorescent light nearly blinded him and he closed them at once.

"Good, glad to hear it. Let's just get this over with, shall we?"

The second speaker sounded familiar. Dammit, it sounded like himself.

"There's no sense pretending you're asleep. We're monitoring your brain waves so we are aware you're lucid." The tone was condescending and it infuriated Simon.

He tried his own voice.

"What am I doing here?" It was rough, gravelly. How long had it been since he'd had any liquids?

"You brought this on yourself, EL-One. If you hadn't kept running away, none of this would be necessary. You're flawed. It's to be expected, I suppose."

Simon dredged his lids open one more time and saw his face mirrored back at him. This had to be some kind of mistake. Didn't they know who he was?

"Get me out of here right now!" He wildly cast his gaze around the room, but it was met by pitying looks from men in white lab coats.

He thrashed violently against his bonds, his instinct for survival driving him to fight. Something bad was going to happen, he knew it. Simon wrenched his right arm, buckled down securely in the leather strap.

"Sedate him, now!" His double snarled almost primitively, causing the lab workers a moment of pause. "Never mind, I'll do it myself."

Simon felt cold fear wash over him as his twin grabbed a hypodermic needle and strode to his bedside.

"Sir, that's a triple dose. You can't give that to him, it might kill him," the attendant with the clipboard interjected on his behalf, but received a withering glare for his trouble.

"If he dies, clean it up."

The needle jammed into his hip and the medication burned his flesh. His head was swimming now. He was lost. Darkness was coming for him, maybe for the last time. He fought for each breath, now. It became harder and harder to pull one in. It was almost a relief.

•

Simon sat up in the shadowy room, gasping for air

that came easily. He was disoriented, his head spinning with confusion. He forced himself to inhale slowly, calm his reactions.

It was freezing cold. He was naked.

A light sheen of sweat glistened off his body and his hands still shook from the nightmare he'd just had. Tess whispered something in her sleep and as he looked down at her peaceful face his situation came rushing back.

Oh, God. There she was, next to him. As beautiful as an angel and everything he could want out of his life. But was it his life? Was that just a dream or some terrible memory trying to resurface? Suddenly, he questioned everything.

He slipped away from Tess as smoothly as he could, hoping he wouldn't disturb her sleep. His legs were still shaking from the horrifying experience, and it felt like ice water pulsed through the veins in his wrists as he covered her. She didn't stir again. Who knew when she'd slept last? He'd let her rest for as long as he could while he planned their next move.

The fire was down to glowing coals, but it was enough to glint off the metal case he'd brought through the door with him. It held answers he would need if they were going to get through this. Maybe it held answers he didn't want to know.

He dressed to go outside, picking up the file case before opening the door. A little fresh air would clear his head and the daylight would be easier to read by. Once he closed the door securely behind him, Simon stepped out into the vast forest. Thick pines clotted the sky with their heavy branches, forming a natural roof over his head and blocking out what dim morning light the winter sun cast.

ATV trails ran off into the distance, but they hadn't been used in a long time and were barely discernable with all the debris from the trees covering them. Simon skirted the perimeter to make sure they were the only people in the area before he cautiously picked his way back. There was a stump out behind the cabin. He'd seen it last night when he picked up firewood, and if he could pry the rusty axe out of it he would have a place to sit while he read Sophie's file.

Their little shack was near the top of the mountain, but completely covered by the thick foliage and couldn't been seen from the air. Simon hoped it hadn't been a mistake to light the fire. It was something he had never dared to do for his own comfort, but he wouldn't allow Tess to suffer if he could help it. It could give them away, though, if anyone was even looking. He'd have to be extra vigilant.

He placed his thumb on the biometric scan pad and the mechanism clicked. Simon spread the file open on his lap but discovered he was hesitant to read its contents. He couldn't let this irrational feeling of dread take over. Tess was counting on him, and most likely Sophie, too. He was going to have to put his emotions aside and view this information with clinical detachment. He could do that.

The first pocket on the left side of the jacket contained hand written notes. He pulled them out carefully, balancing the case with his elbows as he brought the papers close to his face. The writing was sloppy, but legible if he squinted. What he saw there didn't make sense, however.

They were admission notes from the physician on

staff at Rose Medical Center in Denver, Colorado. The pages detailed a car accident with two patients, Sophie Bennett and her husband, Ryan Bennett. Apparently both had suffered brain damage and the facilities at the hospital weren't capable of treating them. The last page outlined procedures for having them transported to Poly Tech, where they would undergo a breakthrough medical technique that could save their lives.

This was crap! Simon knew this was a cover story and he'd bet his life it was the one Trudy believed as well. Laconia had Tess's friends snatched right out of the hotel and probably sedated them for the trip in. But the real question was what they did to them when they got there.

He reached inside the second pocket and pulled out a handful of typewritten forms. It was all there in black and white and Simon's head reeled when he read the first line.

Subject: Sophie Bennett
Imprint ID: SB-ONE
Notes: SB-ONE was fabricated in a facilitated process due to the extreme nature of the injury to Subject: Sophie Bennett. Although her imprint has provided valuable insight as to the workings of the original bio subject, we find the imprint model is unable to retain proper memory recollection and emotional control. SB-TWO is currently in imprint phase and we expect a stable result once the proper production cycle is complete.

The pages slipped from Simon's fingers and he felt a ball of nausea seize control of his stomach. The imprint was Sophie's clone, but that wasn't what tore him apart inside. In Simon's dream, Laconia had referred to him as EL-ONE ... Emory Laconia One. He wasn't a fool. He could see the correlation.

Oh Jesus, I'm a copy. I'm less than nothing! Then I have nothing to offer Tess. Simon pressed his palms against his eyes and doubled over. *I'm some kind of mistake that got away. That's why I have holes in my memory and I'm driven to do all these things I can't understand.*

It was true. It had to be. The evidence he'd been searching for since he woke at the hospital was right in front of him. It was all some big joke, what he thought of as his life... he'd probably been designed to come back to the facility where he was created, and that's why he was here now.

How could he help Tess and her friends if he couldn't help himself? He wasn't even a real person. This left him with nothing to hope for, and she deserved better than a fake. He would turn himself in at the facility. He was just thankful he hadn't put her in any more danger than he had by involving her in his delusions and false memories.

Simon retrieved the loose pages on the ground and slipped them inside the case, snapping it shut. He had no idea how a copy of a real person could feel so much pain at the thought of losing Tess. His heart felt like it was tearing apart. He wouldn't tell her, not at first. Just go inside and use the cylinder to get her back to the facility. She'd find out soon enough, anyway.

He noticed the lack of sound in the forest a moment before everything exploded around him. Shouts echoed off the mountainside, only to be drowned out by the approaching helicopter that whipped the branches of the pines overhead. They were coming from the front and they hadn't seen him yet.

Simon steeled himself for capture. He was already resigned to giving himself up, but he couldn't swallow the idea. His instincts told him to back into the forest, blend in with the trees and watch from a distance. He couldn't let go. The need for survival pulled his feet away from the cabin and into the woods. He didn't know who he was, or even what he was. But for the moment he loved Tess, and he was free.

•

The fire was nearly out. The air in the cabin was chilly but Tess didn't stir beneath the blanket. The delicious scent of Simon's skin covered her from head to toe and she took a moment to savor the memory of their lovemaking the night before. She was a little upset over the fact he wasn't next to her at the moment, but if he was out gathering firewood she'd accept his excuse. He'd have to make it up to her, of course. And she knew just how.

She thought she heard a noise outside, a pulsing thud in a pattern that she wasn't able to identify. It got louder by the minute and she could feel the concussion in the air. She sat up, clutching the blanket to her bare chest. There was no sign of Simon in the cabin and no doubt the sound she heard was a helicopter in the distance.

Tess pulled on her clothing as quickly as she could. She took stock of the items around her, none of which included Simon's clothes or the silver case he'd brought with them last night. Did they have him already? She didn't think he'd leave her alone if he didn't have a choice.

There had to be a knife in the kitchen, something she could defend herself with. It was stupid, she knew. Whoever was coming probably had Death Rays and who knew what other technology. It didn't really matter as long as she felt like she had something. The last thing she was ever going to do was go down without a fight.

The door flew open before she got her hand in any of the drawers. Splinters of wood shot across the tiny space inside and a bitterly cold gust of wind stirred up a grey cloud in the fireplace. Tess choked on the ash, orange embers dancing around her feet as they settled onto the polished hardwood floor.

The doorway was crowded with men dressed in black. They glanced around the area though it was pretty obvious she was the only one there. After a brief nod, they moved aside and another figure came in. Tess's heart jumped into her throat. God, he looked so much like Simon. It wasn't though. She could feel it when she looked into his eyes.

Emory Laconia gazed at her with genuine concern. He rudely pushed a man out of his way and strode toward her with purpose. She saw the look of surprise on the faces of the men inside, but they covered it up quickly. Emory pulled the leather gloves from his hands and Tess braced herself for what was coming.

"Thank God he didn't hurt you." He ran his bare fingers across her cheek in a tender gesture and she repressed the shiver of revulsion that climbed up her spine. It wasn't what she expected, and she was relieved. If they didn't know what Simon did to her, they probably didn't have him in custody.

"Simon would never hurt me," she declared with defiance, looking him in the eye.

"Oh, is that what he's calling himself now?" Emory barked out a laugh. It was abrasive to her ears. Tess realized she'd given away a part of her hand, but they'd find out she was with him sooner or later. She believed in Simon and it gave her strength to stay true to her feelings. From now on, she'd play it smart. Emory wouldn't get a rise out of her again.

"It's not your fault, my dear. I blame myself, really. If I had been more open with you about what Poly Tech was doing, you wouldn't have been so mislead. I just wanted to make sure you were ready for everything I had to offer." She watched out of the corner of her eyes as he slipped his right hand into his coat pocket.

Everything he had to offer? Tess found that statement disturbing. She was pretty sure what it was he had to offer her. Still, it was best to play along and that was exactly what she needed to do.

"I know you will tell me everything. I'm so glad you found me here. I had no idea how to get back." She silently prayed her voice was sincere. It wasn't easy.

"Tess, are you alright? You look a little pale." Emory took a step closer and placed his arm around her shoulder.

"I feel fine. I don't know what you mean." She tilted her head up to look at him when she felt his bare fingers on the back of her neck and she frowned in his face. It was too late. The needle pricked the skin below her hairline and her legs buckled.

"I think she's fainted!" He exclaimed to the witnesses in the room.

It was the last thing she heard as her vision grew dark and she fell into Emory Laconia's arms.

FIFTEEN

They set up a four-point perimeter around the cabin. Simon hung back in the shadows deeper inside the trees. The helicopter couldn't have touched down on the top of the mountain; it must have landed in the dry lake bed just over the ridge.

They were taking her away and he was letting them. The thought twisted his heart, but he couldn't dispute the proof right in front of him. He still had Sophie's file and everything in it. He hated the contents of the case and what it meant for him.

For so long he'd held onto the sliver of memories that had grown to mean so much to him. The red-haired girl on the lawn playing Simon Says...He had suspected it was Tess all along. He loved that memory, but now he knew the truth. The recollection didn't belong to him. Laconia had the right to everything Simon was, everything he felt. Simon knew that if he loved Tess, Laconia did as well. The implications churned his stomach.

A second group of armed personnel fanned out past the first perimeter and he knew if he stayed longer he'd be caught. And this time, they were looking for him. It was ironic how far he'd gotten into the facility looking like Laconia, and now the very same advantage damned him.

In more ways than one.

Even when he didn't know who he was, he still felt like a real person. He had a purpose to fulfill and answers to seek. This revelation left him empty and lost. The feeling was unlike anything he had experienced before.

His instincts told him to fade into the forest. Bury the file case where no one would ever find it, and disappear. Could he do that? It was possible there was something in the records that could help Sophie. Was he so far gone, a mere replica with no soul, that he would be able to turn his back on them?

He sure as hell didn't feel like it. Maybe he was only a copy, a faded version of someone else, but he couldn't just walk away. He—Simon—had given his word to Tess. If she trusted him, he would be there for her. There was nothing Laconia could do to make him relinquish that promise because, at the end of the day, it really was all he had that was his.

Simon slipped down the hill, treading on thick pine needles so he didn't leave a footprint in the snow. Once he reached a lower ridge he doubled back around the ravine to head north. He knew the way to Poly Tech Acquisitions—or Laconia did. Either way, it didn't really matter.

As long as he got there.

•

Tess had one bad-ass headache. Every time her heart beat it pulsed in her temples with a sickening thud that made her want to throw up. She couldn't remember what she was doing or how she got that way. Tess dredged her mind for answers, but when none were forthcoming, she was forced to open her eyes and look for herself.

The room was almost dark. There was a small lamp on the stand next to her bed and she had a glimmer of memory. It was her suite at Poly Tech Acquisitions. She'd come to town with Sophie and Ryan just yesterday, but she couldn't recall how she got from the hotel to the facility. It was disorienting.

She tried to sit up. A figure on the couch across the room rose and politely coughed. Startled, she snatched the comforter securely around her body. For some reason she didn't understand, Tess felt like she was naked.

"I'm glad to see you're awake, Tess. I've been terribly worried about you." The voice was deep and masculine. He approached her carefully and when he came into the light she saw his face. Dark hair, deep blue eyes...yes, he was familiar.

"I'm Emory Laconia. Do you remember me? I am the head of Poly Tech Acquisitions. At least until you assume the reins, my dear." He smiled and it should have been charming, but she couldn't warm up to him.

He called me my dear. How well do I know him? What am I forgetting?

"I'm sorry, Mr. Laconia." Tess didn't want to appear rude. He certainly did ring a bell with her. Perhaps if she played along for now she'd learn more. "I have an awful headache, so please excuse me if I feel a little out of it."

"Understandable. You've been quite ill since you arrived two days ago. We've let you sleep but your friends are anxiously waiting for you to feel better." He sat on the end of the bed, then. As he appeared to be comfortable doing so, she said nothing about it.

"Oh, Sophie and Ryan are here? I can't even remember what I was doing last when we were all together." It had something to do with drinks in a bar. And candle light?

She was a mess. It felt like her memories were all in pieces and she had to put them together. And she'd been here two days. What had she caught, anyway, the plague? It felt like it.

"I thought it would be nice for all of us to gather on the veranda for a welcoming dinner. What do you think, Tess? You must be hungry by now."

She wasn't sure how hungry she was, but she wanted to see Sophie badly. Every time he mentioned her friend she got an unsettled feeling in the pit of her stomach. Something about this felt surreal, but she couldn't put a finger on it. It could just be her illness, though.

"Okay, let me get dressed. You don't have to wait. Just tell me where to go and I'll meet you all there." The last thing she wanted was to have him hanging around when she was getting ready.

"As you wish, of course. Go down the main stairs on the landing outside your room. When you get to the bottom, walk back through the corridor behind them. You'll find us through the kitchen, on the patio." He nodded, watching her intently.

His instructions made her dizzy. She'd done this before, she was sure of it. But if she had, she didn't remember it. Everything around her seemed a step out of sync.

"Don't worry," he gave her that sweet smile one more time. "This will be fun, a fresh, new start for everyone." A fresh start? Did he mean at Poly Tech? The entire situation felt strange, but she knew she was supposed to be there. It was what her parents wanted and from what Mr. Laconia said, her friends were fine and waiting for her. Sophie was probably worried half to death by now.

"It sounds good." As he walked to the door she realized she failed to express her gratitude for what he'd done. "Mr. Laconia? Thank you for taking care of me when I was sick. I really appreciate it."

"Oh, Tess," he breathed the words out with unusual intensity. "Please call me Emory. And you should know I will always take care of you."

She hoped not. Tess locked the door but she had no illusions about the fact that Emory Laconia could enter any room he liked. He was there when she woke up, after all. She'd probably never be able to sleep in this place.

The warm water relaxed her and went a long way toward easing the pain in her head. All her clothes were neatly hung in the closet, though she couldn't remember doing it. She felt refreshed and a little silly about all her reactions a while ago. Emory Laconia had been perfectly kind and done nothing to warrant her suspicions. She should remember her manners and make an effort to be friendly as well.

Her feet took her down the stairs and through the corridor before she needed to recall the directions.

Tess could hear voices as she entered the kitchen. Sophie's laughter stood out and she sounded happy. Her shoulders relaxed and she wondered why she'd been so stiff. Everything sounded fine, and as long as she was letting down her guard, the food smelled pretty good too. Maybe everything was okay after all.

She'd seen the veranda before. She was certain of it.

It was underground, like the rest of the facility, but set up like a garden. It felt like she was outdoors.

"Tess, there you are! Oh my gosh, I've missed you!" Sophie jumped up from the table and disengaged her hand from Ryan's before Tess could dwell on the familiarity of the atrium. Ryan waved at her with a smile, but his eyes followed Sophie with adoration as she dashed around the chair and threw her arms around her friend.

"I'm happy to see you, too. So, everyone here is fine?" Tess felt foolish for suspecting danger at every turn. It was obvious by the love-struck look in Ryan's eyes and the satisfaction on Emory Laconia's face that all was well.

She was over reacting and she didn't know why. In fact, she felt a little ridiculous as she chose a seat next to Sophie on the other side of the table. Tess retained the feeling her friend wasn't well, but it sure didn't look like it.

"So, Sophie, you feel better too?" She threw the question out there, but it was Ryan that answered.

"I know we were worried about her when we first got here, but then everyone had a good night's sleep. I think I slept for a whole day, actually. But when I got up this morning, there she was—perfect and good as new."

"Nobody's perfect, love," Sophie laughed and favored Ryan with a wink. He blushed and it all seemed normal. So there she was again, alone while the two lovebirds cooed next to each other at the table. Or was she?

"May I take this seat?" Emory placed his hands on the back of the chair and smiled at her. Her heart beat faster when he did that, but she didn't know why. The sound of his voice, the way he looked in her eyes, it excited her. Yet the man himself made her want to shy away. It didn't make sense.

She needed to get her bearings and she was very worried she'd forgotten something important about this person next to her. He was clearly fond of her, and as the evening wore on it became apparent they were involved in some way. Tess had no idea how that could happen after being here such a short time.

"If it's okay with you, Tess, I think Ryan and I are going to go upstairs and talk for a while before we go to sleep." Sophie stood and offered her hand to their shy friend. It was unlike her to be so forward, but Tess thought maybe she was just tired of waiting for him to make a move.

"Sure thing." She was actually glad for the excuse to call it a night. Emory's attentions were a little over-whelming and she still wasn't feeling like herself. "I'm a little chilly, now that you mention it. I think I'll go up-stairs, too."

"Oh, I was hoping you'd have a nightcap with me be-fore you turned in. I'll stoke the fireplace for you." Emo-ry was quick to put his hand behind her chair before she could slide it out. Sophie gave her a knowing look and left the room with Ryan. It seemed like she was stuck for a little while longer.

"That's fine. Thank you for asking." When she agreed, Emory pulled the seat out for her and walked her over to a couch close to the fire. It was warmer next to the flame and she felt more comfortable.

Emory kneeled down, pulling the poker from its holder and leaned back on his heels as he prodded the flame to life. Tess felt a sharp flash of déjà vu wash over her and she had trouble catching her breath. Her heart ached.

He straightened and sat next to her on the coach. Her emotions were so out of control she didn't try to stop him when he tenderly took her hands.

"Look at me, Tess. I know we've only been together a short time, but there's something I need to tell you." His voice rang in her ears, she'd heard these words before but they were all wrong. She closed her eyes and a picture flashed in front of them—a passionate kiss with a man. It was Emory—but it wasn't. This wasn't right!

"Stop!" Tess jerked her palms from his grasp and stood up. "I don't know what happened to me, but I do know I don't want you to touch me. Stay away from me, I mean it."

"Please, calm down. You love me Tess, don't you remember?" He stood to face her, his hands spread open.

"Like hell I do. I don't care if I ever remember. I already know what I feel for you."

"It's him, isn't it?" Emory's breath hissed out in a fury. His tone was laden with pure hate and Tess took a step backward. "I think he's calling himself Simon these days. I should have killed him when I had the chance."

Simon! That name, she knew it. She felt something. She saw his face in her mind—the same as Emory's, but as different as night and day. She loved Simon.

"I gave you a second chance, Tess. A fresh start and you still let him ruin it." His hands balled into fists and the vein in his temple throbbed. "The damn memory wipe worked well enough on Ryan, it should have worked on you, too. I can see why it failed with Sophie, her attachment to you was strong, but you only knew Simon for hours!"

"What are you talking about? You're crazy! I just saw Sophie and she's fine."

Tess's head was spinning. What had he done to Sophie? He said he erased her memory, but was that even possible?

"Do you really want to see Sophie? Do you want to see everything I've done for you, Tess? Come with me now."

He grabbed her roughly by the arm and she struggled against him until she freed herself. "I can walk without any help from you. I told you not to touch me." He nodded curtly and moved to the door.

"You will love me, Tess, one way or the other. And I'll show you why."

Sixteen

Simon hoped he wouldn't need to hike all the way to Poly Tech. It would be tough to make it past security, even if he got that far. What he really needed right now was a good, old-fashioned door. One with a knob that turned. There weren't a lot of those out in the forest, but he was bound to come across an old shack or a power station eventually.

It had been hours since the incident at the cabin that morning. He was forced to stick to ATV and game trails on foot. He didn't dare walk the road and lose the advantage of the overhead foliage that covered his progress. He'd heard another helicopter, probably several, no less than half an hour ago. They were still looking for him and they wouldn't stop—he was a valuable commodity.

Quit thinking like that. There's only one thing that matters right now and you have to keep your focus if you're going to be any help to her. All Simon could see was Tess's face, everywhere he looked. It kept him going, kept him ahead of the search team.

A motor revved in the distance. Simon froze in his tracks and listened carefully as it grew louder. He scrambled off the path, landing in a thick pile of brush that concealed a twisting vine of brambles. They tore his coat and scratched the exposed skin on his face, but he perversely welcomed the pain. It let him know he was real in some way.

He could see the trail from his vantage point, low to the ground. It was less than a minute before the ATV came rolling around the corner. It was moving fast, too fast to be looking for him. The driver had someplace to be and if Simon followed, he might find a building or something he could use.

He waited a handful of minutes until he was certain no one was with the rider. Thorns ripped the rest of the way through the fabric of his parka when he stood. Goose feathers floated down to the ground like snowflakes. It looked like he'd be leaving a trail after all. Hopefully no one stumbled across it.

There was sky ahead in the distance. A clearing opened up at the end of the rudimentary road. Simon stepped off the trail and into the thick forest. He used the brush for cover to get a closer look. Male voices echoed off the trees and he heard the sound of one vehicle running. The pale sun glinted off the dull grey metal of a utility building in the clearing.

Three men stood near the door. Despite the dangerous welcoming committee, he was thrilled to see a round, brass knob. The security team leaned over a map, spread out on the seat of one of the nearby ATVs. The wind whipped through the clearing and batted the edges of the paper around. They grumbled and tried to hold the corners down.

"Damn!" He heard one of them spit out as his cup of coffee tipped over and splashed on the map. "Let's go inside. You got the key?"

"Yeah, I got the key. I'm not an idiot like you. You almost got your coffee on my coat, jackass." The second man pulled a ring out of his pocket. It was attached to a retractable string, clipped onto his belt. Simon wasn't likely to be able to get it off him, but he hoped he wouldn't have to. If they went into the building, he'd only need a few minutes to attach the cylinder and slice the door. He'd be stepping into the broom closet at Poly Tech and they'd be none the wiser.

It was a little risky, but it was the best plan he'd come across so far. As long as they didn't see him, he was in the clear. There were no windows in the tiny building and he didn't intend to take a lot of time.

The leader of the bumbling group put the key into the lock in the center of the knob without taking it off the clasp. When the door cracked open it slid back onto his belt with a clack. Someone flipped on the light and they all went inside. Simon waited a minute. The ATV was still running but they didn't appear to care about that.

He crept up to the door and primed the cylinder. He was nervous. The device made a clicking noise and released an acrid odor. Hopefully the sound of the engine would cover it. He attached the end to the cold metal knob and turned the base of the tube.

Nothing happened.

The door was locked! He hadn't considered that possibility. Some doors locked automatically from the outside. And he couldn't disengage. The cylinder wouldn't release until the cycle went through.

"Hey! The door knob just jiggled." A muffled voice shouted inside.

Simon didn't know what to do. His right hand

gripped the copper tube until his knuckles were white. He could run, but he couldn't leave the cylinder behind. Before he could react the door jerked inward, his fingers still on the humming device. The violent momentum pulled him forward and he stumbled through the doorway—into the closet at Poly Tech Acquisitions.

The cylinder sighed one last time and unclenched, falling lifeless into his hand. As far as he knew, no one had ever opened the door from the other side before. He was drawing deep breaths to slow his heartbeat when he realized he had a bigger problem. He was on Sub-Level 3 between the elevator and the lab. Without an access card, he was trapped down below with no way out.

•

Emory paced in the elevator behind Tess's back. The hair on her neck stood on end and she tightly crossed her arms over her chest defensively. She still couldn't remember much from the past few days, but the elevator ride felt familiar and she took what comfort she could from that.

The important thing was he was taking her to see Sophie. Her friend told her at dinner she was going upstairs with Ryan, but that had apparently changed. She would finally get some answers, and she thought Emory had a lot to answer for.

"I don't understand you, Tess." He frowned at her while they briskly strode to the end of the corridor. "There's nothing I wouldn't do for you. I've loved you since we were children. You must feel the same way."

"Just take me to Sophie. That's the only thing I want from you." She looked into his eyes when she spoke and they burned with fury. He looked like he was on the edge, and if he was going over, she didn't want him taking her along. From what little she knew of him, it was probably a long way down.

"We'll see what you want after I've shown you the truth." He scanned his card at the end of the hall and wrenched the door open.

"What is Sophie doing in here? Where are we?" She was hesitant to step through.

"This is the medical ward. Just go inside so you can finally understand what I've been telling you."

"Excuse me?" A small, blonde woman stepped out from behind a counter. She looked at her curiously and then recognized the figure standing behind her. "Oh, Mr. Laconia! It's so nice to see you again. You forgot to bring that file back the other day, by the way."

"What are you talking about? You know perfectly well I never come to the ward." He was already agitated and he turned on her like a vicious animal. "Just get out of my way, stupid girl."

"Oh, I'm sorry. I didn't mean …" Tess could see the tears welling in the girl's eyes and her heart ached for her.

"You don't have the clearance to even speak to me. Puppies are trained better than you." He grabbed her by the arm, much the same way he had done Tess earlier. He squeezed her flesh and the young woman cried out. "Get your worthless presence out of here and do not come back inside. Do you hear me?"

"Let go of her, now." Tess thrust herself between Emory and the girl, wrapping both hands around his wrist and twisting until he was forced to release his hold.

Call security, she mouthed the words silently, opening the door to the lab for the woman to exit.

"If you do, they won't listen to you." Emory had seen

her. His voice was cold and he was suddenly still. The whirlwind of anger had evaporated, but somehow this new demeanor was more chilling. "Take a break. A long one. We don't want to be disturbed."

The petite woman backed into the corridor, her wide eyes on Tess until the door closed between them. At least one person knew she was down here, for what it was worth. She had her key card, but she doubted it gave her elevated access. Without her escort, she was trapped in the subterranean maze. A feeling of claustrophobia washed over her and it sent cold chills up her spine.

"This way." Emory motioned for her to walk beside him as he passed the counter into a small hallway behind the lobby. She caught the sterile scent of antiseptic and bandages. What could have happened to Sophie so soon after dinner that she needed to be brought here?

She glanced up at his face when he reached out to open a nearby door. A crazed look of vindication distorted his features and he swept into the room like it was a grand accomplishment.

The light was dim, the way they keep a hospital room at night. She saw flashes from the equipment at the far end of the room and realized there was an elevated bed in the corner. Her heart sank and her hands started to shake. She knew it was Sophie, even before she reached the figure lying on the bed.

Her friend was pale and weak. An IV ran into her right wrist and Tess saw her cracked, dry lips. Someone had put a balm on the blisters. She looked like she was at death's door. Tess had a flash of memory – Sophie lying at the end of the bed, head in her hands while she cried.

"Oh my God, what happened here?" Tess gripped the metal rail along the bedside. It was the only thing holding her up as she turned to look at the man who'd brought her here.

"You have to understand, Tess. I didn't know they were with you at first." Emory began to pace again, his hands clasped behind his back. "Ryan attempted to gain access to the facility without using the proper procedure. The containment protocols were put in place. We never meant to hurt them."

She couldn't believe what she was hearing. All of this happened because of her? He continued on when he saw the implications of his words in her eyes.

"I couldn't have you realizing what we did to them, now could I? When I saw your face through the security feed at the hotel, I knew you'd finally come back to me after all these years. I couldn't jeopardize your feelings for me, so I had Chelsith enact a cover story for your friends. Ryan was easy, his memory retracted right away. Oh, but Sophie was a different story."

"What did you do to her, you bastard?" Tess could barely speak, the bile from her stomach rose in her throat and she thought she was going to vomit. When he said the name Chelsith, she remembered the despicable man and was terrified by what he might have done.

"I did what I had to, Tess. I told you, I'd do anything for you." The look in his eyes was tender, loving. It repulsed her and she began to covertly look around the room for something to defend herself with.

"Just tell me!" She shouted the words out and a genuine look of pain crossed his face.

"We made an Imprint, of course. A perfect copy.

Well, not so perfect. We rushed the first Imprint through the fabrication process. I couldn't have you running around looking for your friend, now could I? But SB—One proved to be unstable. It almost caused more trouble than it saved me, I thought. Fortunately, we entered SB—TWO into the program at the same time. It had a longer incubation period and you saw the results at dinner tonight."

Her head hurt. Everything was starting to come back to her. Sophie's bizarre behavior after they went missing at the hotel made sense now. And finally, she remembered Simon in her room. Kissing her and telling her they would work it out together.

"You're thinking of him again, aren't you? I can see it on your face. Now that you know the truth, you know it's not possible." Emory stepped in front of her, gripping her by the shoulders.

"What do you mean, it's not possible?" She couldn't follow his logic. How could she? He was crazy.

"I mean this, Tess." He placed the fingers of his right hand underneath her chin and lifted her face so she'd look him in the eye. "Simon is a copy of me. He's nothing. He doesn't even have a real name. If you think you love him, then I know you love me."

"That's not possible, I don't believe you." She shook his hand off and took a step back to think. Could he be telling the truth? The evidence was right in front of her. Oh, no! Simon has Sophie's file. He must have looked at it by now. What if he thinks he's a copy, too, not worthy of me as Laconia says? Tess was crushed at the thought of what he must be going through. She suddenly realized she didn't care if it was true. Her heart was the only thing she could trust and it was still with Simon.

Her emotions must have been all over her face. His eyes narrowed and he closed the gap between them, pushing her into the corner of the room. She felt trapped as he loomed over her in the dark.

"Let's be reasonable about this, Tess. I believe in time you will grow to realize I am the one you truly love. I'll give you another chance. Just think about your friends, after all. They deserve another chance, too. Don't you agree?"

It was a veiled threat and it pissed her off. Tess slapped him hard across the face and she saw her hand-print rise on his cheek. He'd have to kill her before she'd let him intimidate her like this. Either way, he'd never have her.

"You're forcing my hand." He grabbed her by the wrist as she balled up her fist to fight back. "You don't seem to understand. I can make you love me. I can make a hundred copies of you. You'll be in a coma, on a bed next to your friend, while I love you every day for the rest of your life."

"It won't matter." She shrieked as he tried to wrap her up in his arms. "It will just be a copy, it will never be me. You'll never have me!"

"We'll see about that, won't we?" He wrestled with her until he captured her arms behind her back. "We can get started now, really. I don't see any reason to wait."

"Someone will know what you're doing. You can't get away with this forever."

"Oh, really? I have so far." She struggled to break free, but he held her wrists behind her back with one of his large hands. "I'd like to know who is going to stop me."

SEVENTEEN

Simon shrugged off the torn parka and slipped the cylinder into one of the pockets of his black cargo pants. He didn't dare to turn on the light switch and give himself away. That left him combing the shelves with a pen light to see if there was anything he could use in the broom closet. At least he could get out. He remembered it wasn't one of the doors on the lockdown cycle.

He was just considering the viability of a feather duster as a deadly weapon when he heard the soft sounds of a whimper in the hallway. It was a female voice and it sounded heartbreaking. He thought it could be some kind of ruse, but he couldn't stand to hear it go on any longer. With a silent turn of the knob, Simon peered out a crack in the door.

Trudy was about twenty yards down the corridor, slumped against the far wall. Her head was in her hands and her shoulders shook. She was trying to cry silently, but it wasn't working. She was so small and fragile. The more she tried to cover up her cries, the louder they got. He couldn't take it anymore.

Trudy was oblivious to her surroundings. Simon walked right up to her and laid a gentle hand on her arm. Her hands flew away from her face and she yelped. He hoped she would recognize him, but when she did, it got worse.

"I'm so sorry, Mr. Laconia! I didn't mean to make you angry. I don't know what's going on anymore. Please don't hurt me again."

"Hurt you? What do you mean?" Simon was suddenly seeing red. If Laconia had put one finger on this girl he was going to rip him apart. He had to convince her that he wasn't the monster she thought he was.

"Don't you remember what just happened?" She tilted her head and her brow furrowed.

"Trudy, I know this is going to be hard to believe, but I'm not Mr. Laconia. I just happen to look like him." He knew how lame that sounded, but it was the truth. He didn't have time to sit with her over a cup of tea until she understood him.

"It should be, but ..." She chewed her lip and her shoulders relaxed a little. "It was you with the file, wasn't it? Not Mr. Laconia."

"Yes, Trudy! Oh, thank you for being so smart." He was elated that she believed him. "Tell me where he is right now. This has gone on long enough."

"He went inside the lab with Ms. Pelham. She was nice to me, she made him stop hurting me, but I'm worried about her." Her eyes began to tear up again. "I don't know what he'll do to her inside there. I don't think she's safe."

Tess was with Laconia! He had to get to her before something terrible happened. He couldn't put his finger on it, but he was terrified by the fact that she was alone with him in that lab.

"Trudy, you have to call security. I'm going in there

to help Ms. Pelham. Tell them I'm down here, tell them anything you can to get them running. I don't care what happens to me, but she can't be alone in there with him." He began to pace, hoping she would cooperate.

"I can't. You don't understand. Mr. Chelsith is the new head of security. He's Mr. Laconia's closest companion. If he finds out what's going on, he won't side with us. I don't know what to do." Trudy balled up her hands and pressed them against her mouth. She was trying not to cry again.

"Is there anyone else you trust, someone above you in the hierarchy here?" He forced his voice to remain calm. He didn't want her to break down again.

"Oh, yes!" Her eyes lit up. "Dr. Greenfield. He's been here forever and he's always been kind to me. Now that you mention it, he's asked me more than once if I've thought anything was strange around the lab or with the personnel. Maybe he knows something is going on, too."

"Trudy, I'm going to give you the case file back. It's in the closet behind me. I want you to take it to Dr. Greenfield now and tell him everything that's happened. Tell him about me and that the file isn't what it seems."

She nodded eagerly and followed him down the corridor. He walked her to the elevator and after she scanned her card, he held out his hand to receive it.

"I'm going in the lab now. Please hurry as fast as you can."

The doors slid open and she stepped inside. Simon was down the hall before they closed again. Tess was alone with Laconia and she needed him. He didn't care what happened to him anymore. It didn't matter. He held the pass under the scanner.

A sharp, debilitating pain shot through his head and he dropped the card onto the carpet before he could open the door. Simon fell to his knees, gripping his skull. He couldn't see anything around him. This had happened before, when he experienced a memory. He squeezed his eyes shut and opened them quickly.

Simon wasn't in the corridor anymore. He sat at a small table in the lab, looking over a game of chess. His pieces were white and it was his move. He had nowhere to go and lifted his head to smile in concession at his opponent. He saw a mirror image of himself sitting in the opposite chair, playing black.

"Well done, a stalemate again!" A voice above his right shoulder congratulated them and clapped him on the back. The voice was familiar.

"Thank you Dr. Greenfield. It's amazing, isn't it?" He smiled at the elderly gentleman who crossed to the other side and shook hands with his twin.

"And you always do well, EL—ONE. I suppose it's time to put you away, now. Emory and I have matters to discuss." The doctor nodded at him and he stood.

"Could I ask you for a favor?" His doppelganger looked at him. "Could we have one more game of chess, without Dr. Greenfield watching us? It makes me so nervous I can't win."

"I suspect neither of you can win," the doctor answered for him. A look of anger washed over his Imprint's face for a fleeting moment and he felt badly for him.

"It will be fine, Alan. Tell the staff not to disturb us until I come out. I'll be in your office as soon as I've finished." As soon as he spoke the words he remembered what happened next, but the vision continued relentlessly.

EL—ONE came up behind him after everyone had gone. He said he wanted to study the board from the white side, as he'd never gotten to be white. He didn't realize the pin prick on his neck was a needle at first, until his vision grew black and his body slumped in the chair.

When he woke the room was spinning. EL—ONE stood over him, wearing his clothes. He was strapped to the bed where they placed Imprints for study after an exercise.

"EL—ONE. Please, stop this. You don't know what you're doing." His voice was rough from the medication that had knocked him out. He could barely move.

"I'm going to run you through the memory retractor so many times, Mr. Laconia, you'll be lucky if you remember to tie your shoes when I'm done. Now you can see what it's like to be the shadow of someone else's life."

Everything went dark again, his feeble struggles against the restraints useless.

•

As Simon came to in the corridor the realization hit him. He was Laconia.

He was never a copy. He should have been over-joyed to discover the truth, but his victory was bitter-sweet. His Imprint's last words echoed in his ears. He did know what it was like to be the shadow of someone else's life, now. The idea that your feelings weren't yours, your heart couldn't love and you were nothing was dev-astating.

Had they treated El—ONE that badly? He patron-ized him at the very least. God, after that chess game they told him it was time to 'put him away'. It sounded heartless after his own experience.

Trudy's reference to Dr. Greenfield and the idea that Tess was alone in the lab with his Imprint must have triggered the memory. He couldn't let Tess suffer for his mistakes. Her entire life might have been different if he'd never lost control of the project to begin with.

Simon heard the sounds of a struggle as soon as he walked into the lobby. Tess's voice shouted from So-phie's ward and his mind snapped. He sprinted across the room and crashed through the door so violently it splintered on the hinges.

•

"Simon!"

The moment she saw his face it all came back to her. It began with the way he held her on the dance floor of the nightclub and she kissed him for the first time. Em-ory was wrong! Maybe the memory wipe failed because she'd known him for a lot longer than a few hours. She suspected that what she felt for the man in front of her could never be erased, no matter the length of time.

Emory was startled by the sudden entrance and she took advantage of it to break free of his hold. Simon held out his hand and she quickly joined him near the doorway. His eyes were full of emotion as he pressed her tightly against his side. She felt safe with him.

"I knew you would find me." Tess pressed her palm over the top of his hand. "I don't care who you are or what happens at Poly Tech after this, as long as you know I love you. I need you to know that."

"Now you have everything." Emory interrupted their moment and the dim light showed them the hate all over his face. "I used all the company's resources to find you after this last escape. I should have killed you when I had the chance. God knows, I wanted to so many times."

"Why didn't you?" Simon whispered and she was surprised to hear compassion in his voice, not anger. What was going on here?

"I didn't dare! An Imprint can't be made from an Imprint. If I destroyed the original, none of us would be here now." Emory gestured wildly and favored them with a disgusted look.

"What do you mean by none of us? Did you create more Imprints?"

Tess felt his muscles tense up and he wrapped his arm around her more tightly. Did she hear him right? What had he said about the original?

"Simon? I thought ... I mean, he said you were a copy. Not that it makes a difference about how I feel for you, but what's happening?" She turned her head to look at him. He raised his free hand to her face and stroked her cheek tenderly.

"That's what I thought, too. I should have known, Tess. I loved you so much. I didn't know how it couldn't be real. I'm sorry to tell you this, but I am Emory Laconia."

She didn't want him to be sorry for anything. She couldn't imagine what he'd been through. To spend so much time hating one man, only to find out he was him. And all the while he fought for her love, not knowing who he was.

"Now you know the truth about him ... and I see the truth about me." Emory spoke softly and his voice was heavy with defeat. "You didn't love me, Tess, because I wasn't real. You knew the difference no matter what I tried. All this time I thought I'd show the world I was a person, too. But all I really did was carry around his feelings and memories for him like a briefcase."

Was he a monster? She had to consider the things he'd done to her friends—to her. Somehow, her heart ached for him anyway. It was the first time she'd felt sympathetic toward him since the night they'd met. She found herself wondering what would happen to him now.

The door to the lab opened and closed. Tess turned to see Dr. Greenfield coming through the lobby. He held a silver case in his hand, like the one Simon brought to her room. She remembered how kind the elderly doctor was to her the night she was at the sheriff station and he'd given her his green smoking jacket to wear. She trusted him.

"I apologize, Mr. Laconia." He spoke directly to Simon before he made it to the doorway. "I should have known all along. I suspected, but had no proof. When EL—ONE hired Chelsith as his new head of security it became very difficult to get near him and to obtain details about his projects. Don't worry; I've had Chelsith taken into custody. He's not talking now, but after a lengthy stay with a few of my old friends at the DOD, I suspect we'll learn more about what went on here."

Tess still thought of Simon's copy as Emory. She couldn't help it. And she saw the look on Emory's face when the Doctor spoke. He talked about him like he wasn't in the room. Simon noticed it, too and a painful realization filled his eyes. He walked over to his Imprint and put a solid hand on his shoulder.

"Alan, why don't we let EL—"Simon stopped in mid-sentence and shook his head. "You know what, let's call him Eli. Let's take Eli upstairs and let him get some rest in his suite until we get this all figured out."

"But, it's not my room. It belongs to you." Eli hung his head and his shoulders sagged. "Just put me away, like you always do."

"I'm not really interested in those rooms, anymore. I've got other things on my mind right now." Simon nodded to the doctor. Two men in white lab coats followed and carefully took Eli away.

"Dr. Greenfield, is that Sophie's file? Is she going to be okay?" Tess couldn't completely relax until she knew her friend's situation.

"Well, my dear, I went over her paperwork and she'll be perfectly fine. He basically put her to sleep so she wouldn't tell on him. It's always easier to retract the memory of a copy and that's what he did. I've already called for the staff to come in and bring her around."

"And how is Ryan taking all this?" She hoped he wouldn't let everything that happened with the Sophie clones ruin the chances of a possible relationship with the real thing.

"Ryan's been told just enough so that he doesn't panic until you two go upstairs and handle the situation." Dr. Greenfield answered her matter-of-factly.

"Wait, we're supposed to handle this how?" Simon looked down at his torn clothing and shrugged incredulously.

"You are the head of Poly Tech Acquisitions ... both of you, if I'm not mistaken?"

Tess looked at Simon and they both nodded at the same time.

"Then do your job. Ryan's in the dining room, probably not touching any of his food and waiting for you. I'll see you after I get some of this mess straightened out."

"Wow, he's a real slave-driver." Tess smiled.

"I think that's what I like about him." Simon cracked the first smile she'd seen in a long time. It showed her how strong he was and she realized she wanted to be there for him as he recovered his memories. She loved the man he was now, and knew he could only become more impressive in her mind and heart. Tess watched the doctor leave and she realized they were finally alone.

"Are you ready to do this with me?" He asked her the question but it felt like there was so much more behind the words.

"You mean go upstairs and explain things to Ryan?"

"I do mean that, Tess. But I want more. We got into this together and I want to stay together. We weathered this storm because we believed in each other. I need that from you every day for the rest of my life or I really am nothing in the end."

"There's something I have to tell you first." She took both his hands and looked into his eyes. They were full of concern over what she might say. "I don't think I can stop calling you Simon. I can try, but it isn't going to be easy. Will that be okay?"

"Oh God, I love it when you call me Simon." The corner of his mouth turned up and he slipped his hand through the curls on the back of her neck. "Say it one more time, please."

"Kiss me right now, Simon." She stood on tip toe like she had on the dance floor the first night they met. "Kiss me like you did last night and we'll dance like this forever."

Epilogue

Warm sunshine bathed his face and he ran across the soft grass to the garden. She was right behind him—he could hear her giggle in the distance. Without thinking he plucked a rose out of the tangle. A thorn jabbed his finger and blood dripped onto his dress pants. His mother was going to be so mad when she saw but he didn't care.

He spun around, hiding the flower behind his back. He didn't want her to see it. It was a surprise. She skipped over the lawn like an angel, red hair springing off her shoulders in the breeze.

"I didn't say Simon says!" She pointed her tiny finger at him and laughed. "I win!"

He couldn't give her the flower now. He didn't know how to tell her he broke the rules to run away and pick it for her. Instead he let her laugh as he dropped it on the ground behind him.

•

It was dark. He felt heavy, like an elephant sat on his chest and prevented him from moving. The sound of medical equipment surrounded him and he couldn't remember how he got there.

"Doctor, he's waking up."

The voice was sweet, caring. He wanted to see her face, to see if she had red hair.

"Good. Just take your time. No need to rush it." The doctor leaned against the bed, he could feel the pressure. "Can you open your eyes?"

"I'm trying." His lips moved. His voice was rough but they heard him.

"That's great. Now, can you tell me where you are?" It was the doctor again. He must have come close because he could smell peppermint breath on his face.

"Hospital?" He choked the response out. He wasn't completely sure, but it was a pretty good guess.

"You're batting a thousand, my friend. Tell me your name and we've got a home run."

His name? Was this a test? Maybe they didn't know who he was. Some kind of accident or something and he lost his wallet.

"I'm ... I," Oh God, he didn't know! Panic washed over him and he heard his heart monitor speed up.

"It's okay. Everything's fine." The doctor said and he felt a cool hand on his arm. "You didn't have any identification with you when they found you at the harbor. The only thing you had was this band on your wrist. At first we thought it was from another hospital, but the coding isn't like anything in our health network. Does it look familiar?"

The light stung his eyes but he wanted to see the band the doctor held out. His head hurt so badly. He tried to focus on the words and his breath caught in his throat. He could clearly make out the type on the cylinder: *Subject: EL—2*

The recognition of it was like a slap to the face. Were

those initials? His initials? A sharp pain spiked through his head and he clenched the band in his fist. He didn't know if he was remembering or if he was crazy, but something was there.

"I think ..." He hesitated for a moment before he answered. "I think my name is Emory."

KIMBERLY ADKINS

Kimberly Adkins resides in Ohio. She's an avid artist who works with oils, acrylics and water colors. She also spends time song writing and sometimes singing—but only when forced! She has always loved Egyptian lore, as well as science fiction and fantasy. For Kimberly, writing romances is a wonderfully appealing outlet for "magic and passion."

www.KimberlyAdkins.com

CPSIA information can be obtained
at www.ICGtesting.com
Printed in the USA
FFOW03n1612061014
7815FF